GHOST BLOWS A KISS

GHOST BLOWS A KISS

Carolyn Hart

SEVERN
HOUSE

First world edition published in Great Britain and the USA in 2021
by Severn House, an imprint of Canongate Books Ltd,
14 High Street, Edinburgh EH1 1TE.

Trade paperback edition first published in Great Britain and the USA in 2022
by Severn House, an imprint of Canongate Books Ltd.

severnhouse.com

British Library Cataloguing-in-Publication Data
A CIP catalogue record for this title is available from the British Library.

ISBN-13: 978-0-7278-9048-1 (cased)
ISBN-13: 978-1-78029-789-7 (trade paper)
ISBN-13: 978-1-4483-0528-5 (e-book)

All Severn House titles are printed on acid-free paper.

Typeset by Palimpsest Book Production Ltd.,
Falkirk, Stirlingshire, Scotland.
Printed and bound in Great Britain by
TJ Books, Padstow, Cornwall.

To Lisa Seidman who laughs with Bailey Ruth.

ONE

I cherish Emily Dickinson's *If I can stop one heart from breaking, I shall not live in vain.* As a high-school English teacher, I weekly assigned an essay on the meaning of the quote I printed on the blackboard, everything from Erma Bombeck's *It takes a lot of courage to show your dreams to someone else*, to Plautus's *Consider the little mouse, how sagacious an animal it is which never entrusts its life to one hole only.*

Sudsy warm water swirled around my ankles (think Galveston in August) as I enjoyed another lovely day in Paradise, strolling in saltwater and picturing a sagacious mouse. In an academic robe? Or perhaps twirling his whiskers.

'That's a boy!' Bobby Mac's robust shout urged our black Lab Sleuth to retrieve the ball bobbing in the surf. Bobby Mac is as dark-haired and vigorous now as when we met in high school. My husband never met a wave he didn't challenge, a tarpon he didn't chase, or a dog he didn't love. And yes, our dogs and cats are with us in Heaven.

Heaven? Do I hear polite laughter? Or perhaps your glance is dismissive. Rest assured, as you will assuredly rest one day, Heaven exists. Those who deny that reality also scoff at the possibility of our faithful earthly companions joining us. St Francis points out that Heaven would not be Heavenly without all of God's creatures. Edith Wharton's sweet observation danced in my mind: *My little dog – a heartbeat at my feet.*

Heaven? St Francis? Dogs? Cats? Oh yes, and parrots, donkeys, goldfish, and rabbits. I sense bewilderment. Perhaps I should present my credentials. I am the late, as in Dearly Departed, Bailey Ruth Raeburn of Adelaide, Oklahoma, a lovely small town nestled in the rolling hills of south central Oklahoma. Bobby Mac and I arrived in Heaven precipitously when he ignored lowering black clouds to pursue a tarpon in the Gulf of Mexico. A summer storm sank *Serendipity*, our cruiser. We were on the shady side of fifty when we met St Peter. Age, of course, is up to you in Heaven. Twenty-seven was a happy year for me and that's how I Appear, flaming red hair, a skinny face, green eyes, lots of freckles, five feet five inches of curiosity, energy, and, I hope, fun. As e. e. cummings wrote: *The most wasted of all days is one without laughter.*

One moment I was barefoot in sudsy foam. The next I clutched a telegram in one eager hand. The message was a summons, oh happy day, from Wiggins, who supervises Heaven's Department of Good Intentions. The department is housed in a replica of a train station circa 1910, when Paul Wiggins was a stationmaster. Now he dispatches Heavenly emissaries on the Rescue Express to help those in trouble on earth.

I adore Wiggins, though he is a stickler for rules. Yes, there are definite rules (Precepts) for emissaries. I am abashed to admit I sometimes have a problem with rules. I quickly murmured the Precepts aloud, hoping to reassure Wiggins that this time I would honor each and every one. I would. Yes. I would.

Precepts for Earthly Visitation
1. Avoid public notice.
2. No consorting with other departed spirits.
3. Work behind the scenes without making your presence known.
4. Become visible only when absolutely necessary.
5. Do not succumb to the temptation to confound those who appear to oppose you.
6. Make every effort not to alarm earthly creatures.
7. Information about Heaven is not yours to impart . . .

I will posit here that I am not willfully ignoring Precept Seven. I am simply establishing my bona fides. Wiggins would surely approve. He is thoughtful, kind, and *very* proper. He believes in Rules and Regulations. I recalled the last time I recited the Precepts to him. Wiggins sorrowfully pointed out that implementation, not recitation, was the goal.

Wiggins is very much a man of his time. He has firm ideas

of maidenly decorum and circumspection. Decorum and circumspection do not describe me. I am impulsive, outspoken (I booted the high-school football captain from my class. You have to live in Oklahoma to understand the enormity of that offense) and I am perhaps a tad reckless. I do try to honor the Precepts. I always intend to honor the Precepts, but the results, to be generous, are mixed, so the telegram in my hand was a thrill. Wiggins was calling on me despite any misgivings he might (oh, all right, surely does) harbor.

I immediately transformed my appearance. Gone was the cream hibiscus-patterned swimsuit, replaced by a green silk top, ankle-length gray skirt and respectable two-inch black heels. I suppressed a slight shudder, but Wiggins equates fashion with frivolity. I almost added oversized horn-rim glasses, but I have my limits. I checked the message: *Great peril. No time to lose. Come posthaste.* I waggled the yellow sheet at Bobby Mac, who understood at once.

I arrived immediately at the replica of Wiggins's train station. In Heaven you simply wish to be there and you are. Travelers thronged on the platform. A languorous blonde in a magnificent 1940s evening gown, a gorgeous shade of lavender, gave me a sweet smile as I brushed past. A seventeenth-century English Cavalier sporting a scarlet feather in his black felt hat looked at me, his dark brown eyes admiring. I flashed an appreciative smile. Some verities are constant, whether in the sixteenth or twenty-first century. Men admire women. As Shakespeare elegantly wrote: *So long as men can breathe or eyes can see . . .*

Suddenly Wiggins was at my side as thundering wheels and a deep-throated whoo announced the arrival of the Rescue Express. A stiff blue hat with a small black brim perched on Wiggins's thick reddish hair. A walrus mustache adorned his florid face. He wore his usual high-collared white shirt with arm garters between elbow and shoulder. A thick black belt, aided by suspenders, supported heavy gray flannel trousers. His sturdy black leather shoes glistened with polish. But he lacked his usual aura of orderliness. 'Jump right aboard.' He took my elbow and helped me up the steps. 'No time for a ticket. Imminent peril. Dark water. Do your best.'

I knew my destination. I always arrive in present-day Adelaide, Oklahoma. I adore my hometown, but hope someday Wiggins might send me to Paris or perhaps Tahiti. But as St Therese of Avila wisely advises: *Trust God that you are where you are meant to be.*

I was scarcely aboard when the Express roared from the station. Clutching a handgrip, I looked back at the platform. Wiggins called out, 'The water is cold and deep. I'm afraid—'

The Express lifted into space. Wheels clacked on the track. I felt a sense of urgency. I didn't step into a compartment, but stood at the doorway, willing us speed. Faster. Faster. No time to lose.

I was familiar with the breathtaking swoop to earth, but this time stars whirled past in a blur. It seemed only an instant and the conductor was at my elbow. 'Next stop, Adelaide.'

The Express whooshed to a halt.

I moved to the door. *Imminent peril.* I must hurry and this time I would follow the Precepts. An emissary has the ability to be present or not. Wiggins expects behind-the-scenes efforts. In past adven—missions, perhaps I Appeared sometimes. Oh, well, to be honest (a Heavenly virtue), I was rather more on the scene than not. In my defense, sometimes I was sure my physical presence was imperative to put someone at ease or to further the mission. But this time I would be the perfect invisible emissary. I felt a pang of regret. I love gorgeous clothes. Wearing a stylish outfit I can't see is like champagne without fizz. This time I would sacrifice my delight in fashion and remain unseen. I would make Wiggins proud. I would simply take pleasure in knowing my clothes were gorgeous without seeing them. No sacrifice was too great. To boost my spirit, I switched from the prim costume donned for Wiggins's benefit to a paisley blouse with swirls of red and blue and sil—

'No time to dawdle.' The conductor's tone was urgent.

I swung down the steps into darkness and shivered as a north wind gusted. I immediately changed into a snug navy cashmere pullover, gray wool slacks, and knee-high navy boots. A navy wool jacket was a perfect buffer for the wind. I added amethyst buttons for a colorful accent. I wasn't visible, but I knew the brilliant color was there.

The Express pulled away, cinders sparking, wheels rumbling. The scent of coal smoke faded. I stood on a path amid a cluster of trees. A crescent moon was scarcely visible through leafless limbs that creaked in the wind.

'Yip. Yip. Yip.' A shrill bark shredded the night silence.

Thankfully an emissary can move immediately from one place to another. I thought *Dog.*

'Yip. Yip. Yip.' A canine shriek.

In an instant I hovered above a pond in a clearing at the base of a hill. The woods were behind me. Lighted windows glowed in a house atop the hill. Garden lights framed steps in a stone stairway leading down from a terrace, but the only illumination at the pond was a single lamppost next to the wooden dock.

'Yip. Yip. Yip.' A small dog trembled at the edge of a wooden floating dock. 'Yip. Yip. Yip.'

A dimly visible figure thrashed in the water a good six feet from the dock.

The dog teetered on the edge of the dock, 'Yip. Yip. Yip.' The frenzied barks bristled with irritation and bravado. With a final high yip, the dog jumped into the water, untended leash trailing behind. Quickly a small head popped up. As the dog swam, the struggling figure slipped beneath the surface. The dog never hesitated, went down in pursuit.

I hovered just over that spot, ready to plunge into the pond. The surface rippled. The dog's head emerged. I was close enough to see the dog tugging a coat sleeve, straining to pull the burden to shore.

I grabbed a sleeve of the coat. Without a sound its wearer rolled to one side and was gone. I held one empty sleeve, the little dog gripped the other sleeve in his mouth. The weight of the soggy coat slowly pulled the dog down.

I let go of the empty sleeve and dived. As I arched below the surface, I gasped at the icy cold of the water. I stroked down, down, down, shed my clothes and boots for a wet suit, instantly felt warmer. Dark, so dark. I made sweeping motions with my arms. My right hand brushed the dog. I grabbed his ruff. My left hand touched an arm, a woman's arm. I seized her and held tight. I tried to remember my son Rob's lifeguard manual. Something about a vise grip. I maneuvered below and behind her, slid my left arm around her. My right hand held tight to the dog's collar. I kicked the three of us to the surface. She thrashed weakly, trying to break free. I instructed in my back-of-the-classroom-ignore-me-and-you-are-expelled-forever voice, 'Go limp. I've got you. Go limp. Go limp.'

Still kicking, I propelled us toward the dock. Only a few feet more. One foot, another. Breathe. Kick. We reached the end of the dock. I kept a firm grip on the wriggling dog and now quiescent woman. I clutched at the edge of the dock with my left hand but my arm still encircled her. I alley-ooped the dog, along with the heavy wet coat, tenacious beast, up and on to the dock.

Now I could focus on the near drowning victim. I held to the dock with my free right hand and pressed her close to the boards. 'Breathe. One, two, three. In. Out. Deep down. In. Out.'

She leaned against me, rasping for air, shoulders heaving. She was thin and wiry, about my height, but skinnier.

Back-of-the-classroom voice. 'Keep breathing. In. Out.'

Gradually the gasps eased and her breath came more evenly. 'Brrr.' She shivered. The water was cold. She was cold. I was cold. I maneuvered her closer to the dock. 'Let's get you out of the water.' I placed her arms on the boards. 'I'll boost you up.'

She murmured, 'Out.'

I felt her muscles tense.

'One. Two. Three.'

She grabbed at the dock's edge, made a huge effort as I shoved. She tumbled awkwardly up and over the side on to wooden slats.

I saw no reason to exert myself. I simply thought *Dock* and I was out. The wind cut like icy needles. I dismissed the wet suit and was instantly dry and warm in a long-sleeve blue-and-white-striped bateau sweater with graceful ribbing at the yoke, navy wool slacks, argyle wool socks, fleece-lined boots. I added a tassel necklace of navy and white beads with a few pink beads for dash. And the lovely navy wool jacket.

'I'll help you up.' I reached down, gripped her arm.

She came unsteadily to her feet, twisted her head to look at her forearm where my fingers were firmly planted. She half turned to stare groggily at the pond, her face squeezed in befuddlement.

A few feet away the dog gave a low growl as he wrestled with the wet coat.

I let go of her and donned my jacket. Navy absolutely favors redheads. For a moment I was distracted, considering colors. Purple was always good. And cream. And jade. And . . . I brought myself to heel. Speaking of, the dog's growls intensified. Perhaps he smelled some pond creature from the coat's immersion in water.

The woman glanced again at her forearm, now free of my grasp. She shook her head as she struggled to understand the inexplicable. She scanned the dock and the pond, empty except for her. She was a pitiful sight in the scant light from the lamppost, hair plastered to her head, sopping turtleneck sweater and slacks clinging to her, short boots. She took a step nearer shore and squished. 'Damn.'

The dog was burrowed under the coat, growls muffled. She swung toward him, moved stealthily, pounced and in a swift swoop grabbed him. The coat slithered over the edge into the water.

She watched the coat sink, then put the dog on the dock, holding tight to the leash. 'What a night.' Her tone was bitter. 'Decent dogs come when you call. Or whistle. Not you. Oh no, you run. And run and run. Straight to that damn pond. I was afraid you were going off the dock and I got tangled on the leash and my head hurts and I don't know what happened. Not the night for a swim.' A shiver. 'My coat's down in scum and my favorite boots are a mess.' Keeping a tight hold on the leash, she used her free hand to pull off one boot, empty more water. She put it on, did the same with the other boot. 'My boots will never be the same.' She looked down at the dog, bent, touched his fur. 'How'd we both end up in the water? Anyway, Buddy, it's all your fault. But I've got you now.'

She yanked at the leash and walked unsteadily across the dock to shore. She headed for the woods, still muttering to the dog. 'How'd we get out? It was like someone helped us. But no one's here.' She reached the woods, looked back at the pond and the illuminated steps, then turned to stare at the lighted house at the top of the hill. 'Where is she, Buddy?'

Buddy darted off the path, snuffled in a pile of brush. She tugged and he reluctantly returned. She moved determinedly into the darkness of the woods, pulling the dog with her. Dried leaves crackled beneath her feet. Branches creaked as the wind gusted. Yet the woods seemed very quiet.

As I followed her, I pondered the silence so meaningful to me. No whoo. No rumble of wheels on tracks. I arrived to find a woman and dog in peril. I saved them. Rescue accomplished. Yet I was still here. Clearly she still needed assistance. How splend— Strike that thought. As a good emissary should, I focused on acceptance of grave responsibility. The fact that I was happy as a fire horse hearing an alarm was irrelevant to the task at hand. Her rescue was just a beginning so this was no time to jeopardize my exemplary performance. I had not Appeared. Not once! I was so struck by my excellence I clapped my hands together. 'Yee-hah.' That's Oklahoma for Babe-you-knocked-it-out-of-the-park.

She jolted to a stop, swung to look back.

I scarcely breathed. What was a little yee-hah between friends and of course saving the woman and dog from the pond surely made us friends. I hoped she would decide my whoop was imagined, a by-product of her stressful night. No doubt at this moment Wiggins was nodding approval of my behind-the-scenes effort. Might I receive an Emissary Award for working unseen? A gold star? I felt modest. (Modesty is also a Heavenly virtue.) Perhaps adherence to the Precepts only rose to the level of a silver star. I imagined my graceful acceptance, voice well modulated. I murmured. 'It was nothing, simply honoring the Precepts which I always endeav—'

She stopped abruptly, stood stiff as a telephone pole.

I bumped into her. 'Oh, sorry.' I clapped my hand over my mouth, backpedaled. Do you ever practice out loud? Especially acceptance speeches? Not that I'd given that many. And then to bump into her and exclaim. Oh my.

She gasped, dropped the leash, whirled to look behind her.

Buddy bolted toward a street that sloped up the hill to my left. A lamppost offered enough illumination to see small ranch-style homes on both sides of it.

A car came around a curve.

Buddy was almost to the street.

In an instant I was at the curb. I slammed my foot on the leash, jerking him to a stop. He turned on me, planted his paws, looking outraged. In the light from the lamppost, I had my first clear view of him, a handsome King Charles spaniel, silky black-and-tan fur, still damp but almost dry. His small sharp white teeth bared in a growl. Buddy was a small dynamo of a dog with a high opinion of himself.

She remained in the deep shadow of an evergreen until the car was midway up the hill, then walked slowly toward Buddy, pausing twice to look behind her at the empty expanse of grass and the dark woods. She stopped a scant foot from the dog, gazed down at his leash. The leash jerked on his end, but remained unmoving on the ground beneath the pressure of my foot.

'Caught by a twig? Serves you right.'

When she grabbed the leash, I lifted my foot.

'If I ever get you inside,' she said in a clipped voice, 'as far as I'm concerned, you can stay there forever.' She picked him up, turned away from the street. She took one step, a second, stopped, looked back up the hill at the lighted house, hunched her shoulders in a shiver.

She stood for a long moment, staring. She used her free hand to push wet hair away from her face. I studied her in the light from the street lamp. She was likely in her early thirties. Curly hair in tight ringlets was plastered wetly to her head. Dark brows. Dark brown eyes. Thin nose. High cheekbones. A generous mouth but her lips now firmly pressed together.

An unguarded face speaks volumes. With no awareness of observation, there is no pretense. I was struck by a cast of countenance that suggested sadness and reserve, a determination to keep emotion at bay, a woman who had borne pain and loss.

Clutching the dog firmly, she turned and headed for a brick

one-story house. A small Honda was parked on one side of the drive.

I checked the street sign near the lamppost. Burnett Place. I remembered that Burnett Place curved up to intersect King's Road, home to Adelaide's finest stately mansions. The lights visible from the pond belonged to one of those fine houses.

It was likely that she and the dog came down the hill from those lights. Yet all appeared serene there. I wanted to visit the house that drew her gaze, but first I must see her safely home and be sure I could find her again.

I joined her on the porch. She squared her shoulders, turned the knob of the front door. She stepped into a small lighted foyer graced by a maple side table. A leather shoulder bag lay next to a bronze mail tray.

I was entranced by murals on the foyer walls, tall slender palms and a white-sand beach and clear water with the faintest hint of pale green. I immediately felt in a holiday mood.

Buddy wriggled. She unsnapped the leash from his collar and put him down. He danced away, claws clicking on the wooden floor. She stepped into a dim living room with a sofa, coffee table, several chairs. Light glowed from a floor lamp in one corner but most of the room was shadowy. She walked swiftly to an equally dim dining room, made a sharp right turn into a dark hall.

The dog was at the first door, front paws lifted to scratch.

She joined him, knocked sharply. 'Jennifer.' Her tone was forceful, determined.

No reply.

Buddy clawed the door, insistent, confident.

Another firm knock. No reply. She twisted the knob. The door opened to darkness. She fumbled for the light switch. Soft light from a ceiling fixture illuminated a charming room, queen bed with a cheerful striped spread, two easy chairs on either side of a low table littered with books and magazines. Cream drapes were drawn at two windows. Three walls were a pale gold. A mural on the fourth wall was bright with a Paris scene, likely a street in Montmartre. The bedroom wasn't occupied.

Returning to the hall, she moved in a rush, checking another bedroom, flicking on the light to reveal what was clearly an unoccupied guest room. The last room was a spacious artist's studio with an easel beneath a skylight. A palette held oil paints. The canvas was bright with daubs of orange and yellow and vibrant purple. She hurried back to the dining room and pushed through a swinging door into a lighted, unoccupied kitchen. The sink held unwashed dishes and silverware. She walked to a side door, yanked it open. A blue Toyota sedan sat on one side of the garage. The other space was empty. She closed the door, leaned against it. Her frown was intense.

Frenzied barks sounded from the living room.

She dashed from the kitchen into the dining room.

Buddy was in the foyer. 'Yip. Yip. Yip.'

The front door swung in. A glad cry. 'Buddy, oh Buddy, Buddy.' A slender young woman in a pink sweater, gray leggings and gray loafers picked up the eager dog, held him in a tight embrace. A quick tongue licked at the face buried in his ruff.

Her expression troubled, the woman in the soggy clothes hurried to the foyer, her boots squishing. 'Jennifer.' Her voice held a mixture of relief and concern.

The young woman looked up, stiffened. She was pretty in an understated way, soft brown hair, gentle features, but her young face was drawn and pale. She stared at the disheveled woman. 'My God, Fran, what happened to you?'

'I ended up in the pond. Chasing your damn dog. I was glad when you and Buddy went after Travis. I hoped you'd catch him, soothe him down. But I got worried when neither of you came back. I should have gone home.'

Jennifer stood unmoving, unresponsive, as if she were in a faraway place surrounded by silence. The dog wriggled. She eased him to the floor.

'But I didn't. I went up to the terrace.' The bedraggled woman's gaze was hard, demanding.

Jennifer shifted to stare at the mural of the palm tree.

'You know where I found Buddy.' A declarative sentence, again demanding.

Jennifer fingered the golden beads on a fine chain.

'Tied to the stair railing. Barking his fool head off. My God, why did you leave him?'

Jennifer smoothed a strand of hair. 'I need to go to bed.'

The woman I'd tugged from the scummy water moved closer, stood rigid, face tight, hands on her hips, a scant foot away. 'Jennifer, did you go inside?'

Jennifer leaned down to pat Buddy, who pressed against one ankle, then straightened. She folded her arms across her front, a classic posture of resistance. Her lower lip pushed out.

I recalled a long-ago classroom and a teenage girl unable to produce her homework. Her lower lip pushed out. 'Someone took it.' She repeated her claim over and over.

Jennifer's blue eyes were suddenly vague. She blinked several times. 'I don't know what you're talking about.' Her tone was bemused, puzzled, patient. 'And you sound so harsh. Perhaps it's time for you to go home.' She pressed the back of her hand to her forehead. 'I have a terrible headache. I rested in my bedroom all evening. With Buddy. I went there right after Travis left. I didn't know you were still here, Fran. Anyway, I never left my room tonight. No one can say I did.' She whirled away, left Fran in her drenched clothes, hair wet against her head, standing in the foyer, staring after her.

Jennifer hurried through the living room and dining room, turned into the hall. A door slammed shut.

Fran's face twisted in a tight frown. She took two quick steps, grabbed the brown leather shoulder bag from the maple table, slid the strap over her left shoulder. She looked once more at the empty living room and made an oddly helpless gesture, turning her hands palms up.

At the front door, she hesitated, gave a hopeless shrug. She stepped outside, shivered as the wind gusted, hurried to the Honda in the driveway, slid behind the wheel.

I settled in the front passenger seat.

Fran tossed her purse to the floor in front of me. A buckle scraped my shin. 'Ouch.'

Her head jerked toward the unoccupied seat.

My mouth opened, closed. Reassuring words issuing from empty space would not be helpful.

Fran stared at the passenger seat. Her head twisted as she checked the back seat. She finally turned the key, backed from the drive. She drove fast, hands clamped tight on the wheel.

In the occasional illumination from street lights, she looked tense, worried, somber. As we neared downtown, she slowed on Fulton. We passed a one-story white stucco building. A mural on a side wall featured a massive bison on a hillock in a sea of prairie grass. In my Adelaide days the structure housed a real-estate office. Gold letters on the front plate-glass window announced: Roberts Art Gallery.

Fran slowed the car as she passed a deserted parking lot. She bit her lip, shook her head, then lifted her shoulders and let them fall, as if accepting a fact that she could not change. The Honda picked up speed.

She turned on Main Street. We passed Lulu's Café, dark now. Lulu's was a thriving café in my day and sixty years later still served the best breakfast in town, bacon, grits, hash browns, and scrambled eggs with chives. Thoughts of delectable items from Lulu's menu – chicken fried steak, mashed potatoes with cream gravy, green beans cooked with ham hock – entranced me as we wound past City Park across from City Hall and neared Goddard College, a lovely, small campus spread over several hills.

The residential area near the college was modest with many frame houses, none of them imposing. She took a right on to Carleton Way. Midway up the block, she turned into a narrow drive. A lamppost near the house revealed a charming bungalow. Fran didn't bother with the garage. She parked on the driveway, hurried up the steps to the porch, unlocked the front door. A sleek-furred black cat with glowing green eyes waited in the entrance hall. The cat mewed, a hello, glad-you're-back mew.

Fran bent to stroke the silky coat. 'I know. I'm late.'

Another mew.

'It doesn't do any good for me to say everything's all right. You know better, don't you, Muff. You always know.' Fran picked up the cat, gently nuzzled her neck.

Muff mewed.

'Do you smell pond water? I'll wash my clothes. And me. And maybe I'll learn to mind my own business. Travis isn't a little boy now. He's a man. I can't pick up the pieces if he breaks something. Oh Muff, I should have . . . But I didn't.

Muff, I'm scared.' She pressed her face against the cat's fur, then gently put her down.

She bent, pulled off short gray leather boots, held them for a moment. 'My Bill boots. Oh Muff, they were so beautiful.' She choked back a sob, cradled the soggy boots in her arms. She turned from the foyer into a hallway, carrying her boots. She opened a door, stepped inside. In an instant came the rush of water splashing into a tub.

I stood in an inviting living room, comfortable furniture, the beige sofa bright with stitched butterflies, a chair with gold fabric, another with soft stripes of rose and gray, tables with cut glass and painted vases and framed photographs. Books were stacked on an end table.

I lifted my head to listen.

Water splashed in the bathroom. Muff purred. A wall clock ticked. Branches outside creaked in the wind. There was no whoo, no clack of steel wheels on silver rails, no whiff of coal smoke.

Fran was safely home, but she was scared. What happened tonight at the house high on the hill?

TWO

When Bobby Mac and I were invited to a shindig – evening events were always shindigs when they occurred on King's Road – we took special care to appear at our best. King's Road runs along the crest of a hill. The backyards of the mansions overlooked woods and streams. Most of the homes, as was common in Adelaide, were unfenced. The swath of woods afforded privacy and a sense of country living.

I recalled one night when the publisher of *The Gazette* and his wife held a pig roast for the JayCees. Black-haired Bobby Mac was my handsome guy in a white jacket and black trousers. I felt twenty-four-carat in a sequin-spangled short red dress, sleeveless with a fringed skirt. We tangoed on the patio to loud applause.

The house I sought, a two-story Mediterranean-style, was next door to the scene of that long-ago festive evening. I'd visited this home several times as its owner was an avid gardener and president of the garden club. The house was U-shaped. The broad central portion faced the street. In back a wing extended on either side. The garden club often met in a sun-splashed room at the end of the east wing. The windows overlooked her verdant backyard with blooms almost year round. In the spring, her azaleas were legendary.

Tonight the front of the house appeared unchanged. Light on a post by the front porch revealed the same exterior, a cream stucco. The first-floor windows were dark. Light gleamed in several second-floor windows on the west side.

Fran gazed at this house as she shivered on the dock and again after she picked up Buddy to carry him across the lawn to the front steps of the modest ranch-style home.

The stately house appeared placid. Several cars were parked in a circular drive, a Mercedes, a Lexus, a Honda. Light glowed in a lamppost next to the separate garage set back to the west. There was no hint of drama or excitement. Yet Fran's voice quivered when she spoke to Muff: *I'm scared.*

Fran told Jennifer she heard Buddy barking, found him tied to the railing of the steps. I remembered steps at the end of the garden that descended the wooded slope.

In an instant I stood next to a light stanchion at the head of the steps. I looked at the back of the house and felt an instant of disorientation. The garden was gone, replaced by a paved terrace between the east and west wings. Perhaps the pavement seemed even more shocking to me because the space was starkly illuminated by lights streaming from the ground-floor windows at the end of the east wing, harsh, bright, glaring light.

Jennifer mulishly claimed she and Buddy had been in her bedroom all evening, an obvious lie.

Fran knew Jennifer took the dog and set out apparently in pursuit of someone named Travis. Why did Jennifer tie the dog's leash to the railing of steps leading down the hillside behind the mansion? Why did she abandon the dog?

Several second-story windows were golden oblongs behind drawn shades but, on the ground floor, light from three floor-to-ceiling uncurtained windows at the end of the east wing flooded the central portion of the terrace, leaving only the west wing in darkness. I drew close to the lighted windows and looked inside. In my garden-club days the room was cozy with chintz-covered furniture and a table for tea and several leather chairs facing the fireplace. Now the visible walls all held full bookshelves. Several clusters of chairs were flanked by small tables with reading lamps. A massive cream leather sofa faced the fireplace.

More light spilled out through the open door at the end of the wing.

I glanced at the opposite west wing. There was a dim glow behind the closed blinds of several windows. I remembered a matching door at the end of the west wing, but that door was in dark shadow now and not visible. I could see the back door to the central portion of the house and it was closed.

I gazed again at the open door at the end of the east wing. An open door on a cold November night was odd. The room

appeared to be untenanted. Who would open a door on a cold
November night and leave the room? And why? It was more
than odd. That open door was sinister.

I crossed the terrace and stepped inside. I moved slowly,
cautiously, passing the semicircle of chairs, each with a small
reading table and lamp, and a large table. Arranged neatly on
the surface of the table were several sketches. In the middle
of the wall of bookshelves to my right was a door which, as
I recalled, opened to a hallway that ran the length of the wing
to the front of the house.

I approached the back of the cream leather sofa that faced
the fireplace. A fire crackled. A log shifted and flames danced,
but the room was cold. Likely the door to the terrace had been
open quite a while. I shivered, grateful for the warmth of my
sweater and snug blue jacket. A woman's portrait hung above
the fireplace. Perhaps she was in her fifties. She looked poised
for action, confident, in charge. Observant brown eyes. Blonde
hair in a short cut. Lips curved in a pleasant smile. Her navy
silk dress was understated but elegant, a single strand of pearls
lustrous. She looked ready to move, ready for what a day
might bring. I liked her alert, questing expression. This was
a woman who had been and seen and done. She would be at
ease in a boardroom or at a baseball game. I thought the artist
admired his subject, but was a little in awe of her.

The portrait made me think that her presence would always
bring a burst of energy. Her arrival would change the tone
of the room that now felt cold and inhospitable. The open
door to the terrace and the silence made a gracious retreat
somber.

I felt a ripple of unease, a burgeoning sense of wrongness
about this house and the terrace and the woods below. Why
did Jennifer abandon the dog? Why did she lie to Fran?
Why did Fran tell Muff she was scared? My steps seemed
loud on the parquet flooring. I drew nearer. My gaze was
drawn to a portion of a cushion lying on the floor at the end
of the sofa. Perhaps a visitor unknowingly brushed the cushion,
tipping it to the floor.

I reached the back of the sofa and looked down.

A woman's body sprawled on the cushions. Despite

the crushed portion of the head and the welter of blood, I recognized the woman in the portrait.

I forced myself to walk around the end of the sofa.

Blood stained the cream leather upholstery, speckled the cushions, trickled to the floor. A poker lay on the parquet floor between the sofa and the fireplace. Flesh and bone and tendrils of blonde hair matted the pronged end. I bent and touched a limp hand, felt for a pulse. There was no pulse, would never again be a pulse.

The gentility of the surroundings was in dreadful contrast to that battered skull. I quickly stood, though haste would not matter to her. I had to sound an alarm. I gazed around the room. No telephone. I yearned for the days when a phone, usually black with a receiver sitting in a cradle, would likely be found. Surely somewhere in this huge house I could find a real phone.

A brisk knock sounded on the hall door. I whirled to look. The knob turned.

'It's locked.' A man's deep voice sounded surprised.

Another knock.

In an instant I was at the door. I popped the latch, moved out of the way.

Another knock. The door handle moved again and the door opened.

A tall, muscular young man with dark hair drawn back in a ponytail paused in the doorway. His eyes held the same wild look as a half-tamed horse that might bolt at any instant. Like Fran when she stood alone in her entryway, his expression was unguarded. His uneven features, deep-set dark eyes, prominent cheekbones, large mouth, appeared well controlled but one eyelid flickered once, twice, a third time. He shifted a well-wrapped flat square parcel from one big hand to the other.

A trim woman with short-cut gray hair remained in the hall. She radiated competence, command, certitude. She appeared pleasant, but the tilt of her jaw indicated firmness. I admired the bright pattern of large white flowers on her bronze tunic and her sleek black silk trousers, and bronze flats. Nice.

He gave her a polite nod. 'Thanks for letting me in, Margaret.'

'Certainly, Travis.' The words were quite polite, but there was no warmth.

Travis. Another piece of the puzzle slotted in my mind. Jennifer claimed she went straight to her room to nurse a headache after Travis left.

Travis. Jennifer. Fran. The three of them were together this evening in the small house at the foot of the hill. Travis departed first. Jennifer then came to the top of the steps with the dog. Fran obviously was a guest at Travis and Jennifer's house. Eventually she too went up the hill. Was she searching for Jennifer or for Travis?

Travis held out the package to show the woman who let him in the house. 'Sylvia's expecting me. We were talking on the phone tonight and I told her I had a great new painting for the festival and she asked me to bring it by.' He stepped inside. 'Hey Sylvia?' His deep voice reverberated. 'Hey, where are you?'

He looked to his left and stopped to stare at the open back door. 'Hey Margaret, the door's open.'

She stepped into the room, glanced at the open door, shrugged. 'Perhaps Sylvia's on the terrace.'

'On a night like this?' He strode to the door, looked outside. 'Hey Sylvia.'

Silence.

He turned around, appearing irritated. 'Well, I guess I'll wait for her. I want her to see this painting. I guess I'll put it on the table.' He walked toward the ornately carved mahogany table, put down the parcel. He gave Margaret an exasperated look. 'You know Sylvia. She won't like it if I don't stay. I guess I'll hunker down by the fire, get warm.'

Margaret remained in the doorway. 'May I bring you some coffee? Or a drink?'

He brightened. 'That sounds good. Maybe some of that great hot chocolate you guys have.' He was almost to the sofa. He came around the end, headed for the fireplace. He jolted to a stop, his face contorted in shock, his big body stiffening.

'Oh my God.'

*   *   *

A siren squealed in the distance. Arms wrapped tightly across her front, Margaret stood in the two-story entrance hall at the open front door. Cold air swept inside. Margaret's face was flat with shock. Travis, shoulders hunched, lurked at the far edge of the door, leaving Margaret in the commanding space, perhaps to emphasize that he was an accidental participant in a macabre situation. He moved restively, suddenly peered down at the flat parcel in his big hands. He must have retrieved the carefully wrapped package from the table in the library. Apparently not even the shock of murder made him careless about one of his paintings. His bristly black brows drew together. He took two steps to a side table, carefully placed the package there, returned to the open doorway. He pulled out his cell, spoke to Margaret. 'My wife will wonder where I am.' He tapped a text message, slid the phone in his pocket. Margaret made no comment, looked out at the driveway. A siren rose and fell, louder now.

Behind them twin stairways with elegant wrought-iron railings and banisters curved up on either side of the entrance hall to a broad landing with four potted palms looming over a mahogany railing. A fountain splashed midway between the front door to a huge archway. The room beyond was dark. To the right lights shone in a room beyond another archway.

I stepped out on the front porch. Soon the investigation would be in the capable hands of my old friend (and occasional adversary), Adelaide Chief of Police Sam Cobb and his assistant, Detective Sergeant Hal Price. If you ever watch old movies, snag a title starring Broderick Crawford. That's Sam. Thick thatch of silver-streaked dark hair. Big blunt face. Broad shoulders. Stocky muscular body. I was eager to see him arrive, likely wearing his usual baggy brown suit, observant eyes quick to sum up, a man with an instinct, tough enough to hunt, kind enough to care for the innocent. Hal Price? A young Paul Newman.

The siren gave one last squeal as a patrol car jolted to a stop.

I knew the drill. The first responders corral witnesses, requiring silence until an officer has interviewed each one. Other officers would establish a perimeter. The body isn't touched until the medical examiner completes his examination. Officers then record the scene, photographs, video, sketches, measurements, the careful bagging and tagging of physical evidence.

Two uniformed patrol officers climbed the steps to the porch, a middle-aged man with an impassive face and a lithe, pony-tailed blonde. The blonde's eyes widened as she looked through the open front door at the fountain in the middle of a marble floor and the fancy staircases leading to a landing.

Footsteps and voices sounded upstairs. A woman called out from the landing, 'Is it an ambulance for Dad?'

Margaret looked up at the landing. 'It's not your father, Elise. I called the police.'

A man's hard voice demanded. 'What the hell for? There's no excuse for a siren. That kind of shock is all he needs. I'll handle this.' A tall muscular man started down the stairs, assertive face tight with irritation.

Margaret held up a hand. 'Please wait, Dwight. Something dreadful has happened. Someone killed Sylvia.'

A shrill cry from the dark-haired woman at the railing.

Margaret was clipped. 'Everyone please gather in the living room. I have to take the police to the library now.' Margaret gestured at the officers. 'Come in.' Her voice was shaky. 'Someone hurt Sylvia. She's dead.'

Travis spoke up. 'Mrs Foster and I found her. I brought a painting to show her. We walked into the library and it was cold and we found her near the fireplace.'

'Show us.' The older officer was brusque.

Margaret said quickly, 'This way,' and she turned to lead them across the marble floor toward the east wing and the hallway to the library.

The dark-haired woman leaned over the railing of the landing. 'Sylvia's dead? In the library?' Her voice rose in disbelief.

Margaret stopped, looked up. 'Elise, we don't know what happened. We found her. Now we have to help the police.' She looked unsteady for a moment. 'It's awful. Dreadful. But I have to show them.' She shuddered. 'Wait in the living room. The police will help us.' She moved forward.

Travis looked reluctant, then hurried to catch up.

I was puzzled by the arrival of only one patrol car. And then headlights sped into the drive. A green Honda slowed to a stop behind the patrol car. Not Sam's car. The driver's door opened, a head was visible.

Not Sam.

I scrambled for a name. I knew him, pudgy, thinning fair hair carefully draped over a bald spot, watery blue eyes. Howie. Howie Harris. Detective Harris had ingratiated himself with Adelaide's overbearing buxom Mayor Neva Lumpkin. Seeing the last of Sam Cobb as police chief likely topped her wish list. Maybe second only to a double serving of iced cinnamon buns.

Howie rolled out of the Honda, cell phone in hand.

I was at his elbow, smelled mint aftershave.

'You can count on me, Mayor. I've pared down everything while Sam's been gone. Investigations are short and quick. Lean staff. I've cut down on overtime. I'm at the Chandler house on King's Road. We got a nine-one-one call at eight forty-seven, first car arrived at eight fifty-one.' His voice quivered. Crime on King's Road meant Loch-Ness-size headlines in the *Adelaide Gazette*. 'Reported homicide. Oh hold on, Mayor, got a text here from Shaffer. He and Woodson took the call.' Howie peered at his phone. 'Body in the library. ID'd as Sylvia Chandler, Arthur's second wife. Shaffer says somebody bashed her with a poker. The back door to the terrace was open so it looks like an outside job. I'll get around there and take over. We'll use Maglites, check out the property, but right now it's looking like somebody came in from outside. I'll reassure the family that the murderer's come and gone. I'll tell the Chandlers the mayor's on top of everything . . . Aw, thanks, Mayor.'

No pouter pigeon ever puffed a chest with more delight than Howie Harris as he basked in the mayor's approval.

Another patrol car eased to a stop followed by a red Corvette. Two uniformed officers joined Howie. A tall, dark-haired man in a rugby sweater and Wranglers and boots climbed out of the Corvette. He moved with the grace and confidence of a halfback who would weave his way down any football field.

I recognized Detective Don Smith, who often worked with calm and sensible Detective Judy Weitz.

Howie pointed at the patrolmen. 'Get around back. Looks like Mrs Chandler was killed by an intruder. Check for footprints.'

Detective Smith loomed over Harris. 'Acting Chief.' There was nothing out of the way in Smith's tone, but Harris stiffened. He drew himself up to his full five foot seven, snapped, 'I'll oversee the search behind the house.' He jerked a thumb toward the front door. 'Inform the residents that Sylvia Chandler was attacked in the library. Shaffer said somebody grabbed a poker from the fireplace and struck her, inflicting fatal injuries. The back door to the terrace was wide open so it looks like an outside job. Assure the residents that the investigation is underway and they will be kept informed.'

Smith gazed at him. 'Has an officer sequestered the occupants? Prevented them from communica—'

'Detective,' the tone was supercilious, 'this isn't a corpse in a bar-room brawl. This is the Chandler house. Family members are to be treated with respect and shown every courtesy. By order of the mayor.' The title was announced in a tone of reverence. After a pause, Howie said portentously: 'You may introduce yourself as Acting Detective Sergeant.'

Police Chief Sam Cobb was absent. Was his lieutenant, Detective Sergeant Hal Price, also unavailable?

Smith shook his head. 'Thanks, Howie, but I won't cabbage on to Hal's rank while he's off with the National Guard. Detective suits me just fine.' He turned toward the porch.

Howie called after him. 'Remember, this is the Chandler house.'

'Gotcha.' Smith reached the broad front steps.

'The mayor . . .' Howie began, but Smith was already walking into the entrance hall. Howie glowered for an instant, then, perhaps recalling the mayor's accolades, he smoothed a wisp of hair disarranged by the wind and gave a self-congratulatory nod.

Howie looked at a sidewalk to the left of the house. Rounded shoulders back, he hurried across the lawn. His exit was marred by a slight stumble over a gopher hole.

*   *   *

Detective Smith stood in the wide archway to a magnificent living area. Massive leather and carved wooden furniture didn't look especially comfortable but certainly gave a flavor of medieval Spain. Gloomy tapestries featured long-faced Spanish saints, crusaders in chain mail, and sail-heavy galleons riding huge waves. Wall sconces provided spots of golden light. 'I'm Detective Smith. I'll be getting information from you to aid us in the investigation into the murder of Mrs Sylvia Chandler.'

The dark-haired woman who'd called out from the landing above the entrance hall was immediately on her feet, one long thin hand outstretched. A huge diamond glittered in an ornate swirl of gold on one thin finger. She pointed accusingly at Smith. 'What is happening? Why haven't we been informed?' Her face had all the charm of a wax mannequin and likely was the product of several plastic surgeries, but her dress was gorgeous. Crepe-de-chine silk with a V-neck and wrap effect and swirly dipped hem. Rainbows arched gracefully against a caramel background.

She took two quick steps forward. 'What happened to Sylvia? Who hurt her? Was she robbed? Her jade ring is worth thousands. Have you captured her attacker? Is it a transient?'

'The house and grounds are being searched. A careful survey of the crime scene will begin as soon as the medical examiner completes his examination. We are in the initial stages of the investigation.' He pulled a notebook from his pocket. 'Right now I need particulars about every person present in the house.'

I tried in a sweeping glance to see the face of each person present. But if one of them was guilty of murder, he or she appeared as shocked as everyone present.

'This is terrible.' A slender blonde in her mid-forties shuddered. She looked athletic in blue warm-ups.

The hard-faced man who'd started down the stairs in response to the arrival of the police was now draped in an oversized leather chair, long legs outstretched. His cold brown eyes settled on the blonde for an instant, returned to the detective.

A stocky fair-haired man spoke thickly. 'Like we're in a precinct or something. Sirens.' Plump fingers pushed back a straggle of sandy hair. 'Damn. Sylvia dead. That's cruddy. Really cruddy.' He looked at the dark-haired woman. 'Somebody will have to tell Dad. I guess it's good he doesn't seem to hear us. That would be a hell of a thing, telling him somebody killed Sylvia.' He rubbed a flushed cheek. 'I heard the sirens from my little spot in the dart room. I ran – guess I didn't run – I wobbled upstairs to check on Dad. I thought something had happened to him, but he's OK. I mean, at death's door if you can call that OK. I yanked open the door. His door. Not . . . Anyway, Nursie shooed me away. Anyway, that's why I just got down here.' His worried frown was replaced by a sudden smile as he looked toward the archway. 'Hey, Margaret, come on in. Damn, it's good to see you. He' – a plump hand waved toward Detective Smith – 'said somebody killed Sylvia.'

Margaret and Travis stepped into the grand room. Margaret spoke in a bleak staccato. 'We' – she gestured at Travis – 'found Sylvia's body in the library and called nine-one-one. When the police arrived, we took them there.' She spread her hands wide. 'That's all I know. It's quite dreadful.' She looked at Detective Smith. 'I understand you will speak to everyone in the house. Except for Mr Chandler. He is quite ill. In fact, he is in a coma and not' – a quick breath – 'expected to live much longer.' Her voice was steady but I saw pain and sorrow in her eyes.

The pudgy man spoke with great care, the words only slightly blurred. 'Yeah. And we all thought Sylvia would outlive—'

Elise said sharply. 'That's enough, Stuart.' Her glare was insistent, demanding.

He blinked. 'Anyway, Paps is about to boogie off—'

The fine-featured blonde looked at him coldly. 'Don't call Father Paps.' She jerked toward the detective. 'Why are you talking to us? You should be out looking for the man who hurt Sylvia.'

Margaret said quickly, 'They are looking, Crystal. There are searchers behind the house.' She turned to Don. 'What can we do to help?'

'Please sit down, ma'am.' He jerked his head at Travis. 'Sir.

I won't hold everyone long but police reports require a list of every person in the vicinity of a crime scene.' His tone was pleasant, matter-of-fact.

Margaret walked toward two high-backed wooden chairs. Travis slowly followed.

I looked at him with interest. This evening he'd left the small house at the bottom of the hill and was soon followed by Jennifer and Fran. Yet he arrived at the front door carrying a painting to show to Sylvia. I wanted very much to know if he'd first visited the terrace behind the house.

Margaret sank limply into the second chair, stared blankly forward, obviously distressed. Travis sat in the other chair, his angular face taut and wary, big hands balled into fists.

'Hey,' a trim middle-aged man leaned forward. 'What happened to Sylvia?' He was country-club perfect, from a crew-neck white sweater to a carefully trimmed blond mustache.

Smith spoke in an even tone. 'Mrs Chandler's body was found on a sofa in the library.' He didn't elaborate on the cause of death or possible weapon.

A frisson of horror rippled through the huge room.

The dumpy man with the flushed face blinked several times. He tugged at the throat of a baggy gray sweatshirt and with noticeable effort sat up straighter in an oversized red leather chair. His face creased in bemusement. 'So what are the odds? Super-fit Sylvia dead.' The tone was wondering, as if surely she could not be dead. 'Why she was good to make it to ninety. And now Paps will—'

'Stuart.' The dark-haired woman looked grim. 'Let's keep to the point. We need to help the police, give them the information they need. And then we have to decide whether to tell Dad.' She bit her lower lip. She swung to Detective Smith. 'I suppose it must have been a burglar.'

Smith eyed her with interest. 'Burglar?'

She rushed ahead. 'I told her it wasn't wise to leave the terrace door unlocked, but she always laughed and said she lived on King's Road and the only intruders on our land were deer and raccoons.'

The blonde gazed at the detective with haunted blue eyes.

'I'll never feel safe here again. Sylvia loved the library. She read all the time. That's where she spent most evenings. She liked books about dogs and lions and all kinds of animals.' A hint of a smile. 'She liked animals and oil rigs better than most people. And lots of business books. She knew everything about business.'

Detective Smith asked quietly, 'Did she have any enemies?'

The tough-faced man lounging in the big chair raised a dark eyebrow. 'Enemies might be a stretch. But she cut some sharp deals. Harley Ames sure didn't like her.'

The dark-haired woman gave a dismissive wave. 'Harley's all bluster. Anyway, he's in a wheelchair since that wreck. He didn't sneak through the yard after Sylvia.'

Don was taking notes.

'Carl Kelly threatened her after she fired him.' Margaret's face drew into a frown. 'But the last I heard he was in El Paso.'

Smith spoke to her. 'Tell me about Sylvia Chandler.'

Margaret made a helpless gesture. 'I don't know where to start.'

'Personality.'

Margaret was silent for a moment then said with a tremulous smile. 'If I sum her up in one word it would be forceful. Sylvia was a force, like a high wind or a big wave.'

Elise nodded and Stuart gave a thumbs-up.

'When she walked in, a room brightened. She had a deep full laugh and when she laughed everyone smiled. She could be tough as nails – I've seen her negotiate – one minute a smile, another a steely gaze. She was energetic, willing to take on any job. She loved working, whether she was in a board-room or on a well site or leading a meeting.' Margaret seemed to take comfort from a rush of memories. 'Arthur called me from Scottsdale, oh it must have been fifteen years ago, and told me he'd bought a condo and met an amazing woman, Sylvia Cramer, and he was having dinner with her that evening. They were a great match. He'd been lost ever since Ellen died and Sylvia was perfect for him, smart, hard working. The name of her realty company told you everything you needed to know about Sylvia, Yellow Brick Road Realty. I asked how she came up with the name and she gave that deep wonderful laugh and said, "Everyone wants to walk on the Yellow Brick Road."' Margaret's smile faded. 'That was fifteen years ago. And now . . .' She broke off, pressed the back of a hand hard against her lips.

Stuart pushed up and a little unsteadily crossed the floor, patted her arm.

'I'm sorry,' Margaret murmured.

Stuart turned to the detective. 'Maybe you could do what you need to do and get done. This has been upsetting for everyone.'

It was an Oklahoma male's instinctive effort to shield his womenfolk, not because women are weak but because that's what men do.

Smith spoke quickly, 'May I have your names, please.' He looked at each in turn, the dark-haired woman, the hard-faced man sprawled in his chair, the tipsy man in sweats, the brittle blonde, the man with the tidy blond mustache, the grieving older woman.

The dark-haired woman was brisk. 'I'm Elise Douglas.' She gestured at the big man sprawled in the chair near her. 'My husband, Dwight.'

'Stuart Chandler.' A benign smile. 'If I'd known you were coming, I'd have stuck with Perrier. But I didn't know so I have to admit Stu is stewed.' He leaned forward, his tone confiding, 'I wondered what the hell when I heard sirens. I was tossing darts at the target and tipping a glass in the club room. I thought, Oh God it's Dad and went upstairs. And I've had too much to drink. And now . . .' He trailed off.

Elise said quickly, 'It's all right, Stu. We'll take care of everything.'

Smith nodded at her. 'Do you all live here?' The question was polite. He knew from his surroundings and Howie Harris's orders that he was in tall cotton. For all he knew, the very rich congregated like a pride of peacocks.

Elise shook her head. 'We're family. My father, Arthur Chandler, is very ill and we've come . . .' She stopped, swallowed.

Stu slumped back in his chair. 'Oh yeah, address. I'm of

no fixed abode. Right now I'm staying at the house on Grand Lake. We're all here because Dad's dying. And then to see how everything shakes out about the company. But Sylvia . . . I can't wrap my head around her dying first.'

The big man slouched in the oversize chair took control. 'The police aren't interested in what we're doing here. He needs our names for his report.' He spoke to Don. 'Let's get this over with. My father-in-law Arthur Chandler is gravely ill and we are here as a family. Elise and I live in Dallas. My sister-in-law, Crystal Chandler Pace.' He nodded at the sleek blonde watching with her eyes wide and strained. 'Her husband Jason. They live in St Louis.'

Jason stroked his mustache, looked uncomfortable. His milieu was the club at cocktail hour.

Dwight gestured toward the older woman who sat quietly, her hands laced tightly together. Clearly her thoughts were elsewhere. 'Margaret Foster is Arthur and Sylvia's longtime assistant. Margaret keeps everything running smoothly.' He stared at Travis.

'Travis Roberts.' He talked fast. 'I brought a new painting to show to Mrs Chandler. That's why I came this evening. Then Margaret and I—'

'Right.' Smith cut him off.

Dwight had all the hallmarks of a chairman of the board as he continued briskly, 'According to Margaret, she and the young man,' a flicker at Travis, 'found Sylvia's body. Did someone break in? Have the police completed searching the house? Is there any danger to the family?'

Smith glanced at his phone. 'The house, garage, and grounds have been searched and cleared. There is no one presently in the house other than Mr Chandler and his attendant and those present in this room.'

'Oooh, that's such a relief.' Crystal gave a little whoosh of air.

Dwight stood, all six foot three of him. 'Very well. We appreciate the excellent response by the authorities. This has been a great shock and we all need—'

Stu clapped his hands together. 'A drink?'

'Stuart!' Crystal's cry was appalled. 'How could you?'

'Come on, sis. A drink will help. Let's fuzz the edges, make it easier to get to sleep. Instead of thinking about Sylvia and somebody sneaking inside the house.'

Elise swished from her chair, crossed to her brother, yanked at his arm.

Stuart struggled to his feet. 'Oh hell. I didn't mean anything bad. But I don't want to think about Sylvia. Damn gruesome.'

Elise was firm. 'It's been a long evening. We are going upstairs now.' She gripped his elbow, steered him toward the archway.

'One moment.' Smith's tone was crisp. 'Did you go to the library tonight, Mr Chandler?'

Elise shot the detective a shocked look. 'Of course not. Stuart always wants to take the edge off unpleasantness.'

Don studied Stuart's flushed face. 'Mr Chandler, how did you know the death was gruesome?'

There was another instant of horror in the room.

Stuart pulled free of his sister, approached the detective. 'Gruesome? Yeah, that's what murder is. I saw somebody in an alley once. Been knifed. I kept thinking about Sylvia and how nice she always looked. Somebody hurt her, didn't they? That's gruesome, right?'

Don nodded. 'Yes, Mr Chandler. Her death was gruesome.'

Elise was at her brother's side. 'Reaching for a drink is his way of dealing with something awful. And tonight is awful.' She lifted her head, looked imperious, Elise Chandler Douglas of The Woodlands. 'We will expect a report tomorrow on the status of the investigation.' She gave Stuart's arm another yank. 'We are going upstairs.'

The blonde rose, too. 'It's all hideous. I don't want to hear another word about it tonight. We can't help Sylvia and the police will find out what happened.'

They were all standing now, moving toward the archway.

Detective Smith watched them go, his gaze intent. 'We'll be in touch.'

I was on the landing by a potted palm as they came up the stairs, Elise gripping her brother's arm, her big husband close behind, the blonde and her trim husband. Lagging a few steps behind, Margaret used the banister as if she needed support to climb. Elise stared straight ahead. She no longer looked imperious. She looked hagridden and desperately frightened. Stuart was murmuring to himself, 'In the nick of time, but that's a crime. The nick of time.' The blonde clutched at her throat. Her husband's face wrinkled in a puzzled frown. Then he said sharply, 'Damn stupid, Stuart. Shut up.' Margaret tried to control a shudder, gripped the banister.

THREE

Two crime technicians worked in the library. The body was gone, an outline marked in chalk. A skinny tech in blue coveralls filmed one end of the room. A big bulky bald-headed tech held a sketchpad in one hand. Surprisingly delicate fingers gripped a pencil, drew with precision.

The poker remained on the floor between the sofa and the fireplace. Blood and matted hair clung to the pronged end. Eventually the weapon would be carefully placed in a clearly marked evidence container.

Possibly a stranger entered a mansion in search of loot, grabbed up the poker when Sylvia confronted him. I gazed around the library. Nothing appeared out of order. There were no telltale bare hooks on the walls to indicate a purloined painting. I admired two Monets and a Cézanne. A small silver chest graced an end table. An elegant jade statuette of a dragon reigned atop the fireplace mantel.

Elise Douglas suggested a burglar attacked Sylvia Chandler, a burglar who ignored expensive paintings and silver double eagles nicely framed in an alcove.

I stared at the poker with its grisly stains. I considered what might have happened. A stranger came through the woods, entered the library, walked to the fireplace, grabbed a poker to strike the woman seated on the sofa. Why wouldn't Sylvia scream? Raise an alarm? In my view, if someone entered from the terrace, the visitor was known to Sylvia. That visitor might have mentioned the cold, hurried to the fireplace, used the poker to prod the burning logs. I estimated the distance between the fireplace and the sofa. About five feet. Perhaps she was reading, looked down again at her book and the visitor raised the poker, struck. Or someone who lived in the house entered from the hall, locked the door, murdered Sylvia, exited to the terrace.

My gaze moved to the open door to the terrace. Perhaps the dead woman herself locked the hall door which meant the murderer, known or unknown, entered from outside. Or perhaps the hall door was locked by the murderer who then slipped outside, leaving the terrace door open.

To be fair, the open door might truly point to a murderer who entered from the terrace. Jennifer and Fran climbed the hill tonight after Travis spoke to Sylvia Chandler. Why did he call her? Did he find Sylvia dead then hurry to get a painting for an excuse to return and discover the dead woman in the company of someone such as Margaret? Or was Sylvia alive when he arrived and he agreed to fetch a painting? Or did tall, strong Travis bludgeon her with the poker? Did Jennifer find the body? Something upset her so much that she fled the hilltop leaving Buddy behind.

I believed Fran found the open door, stepped cautiously inside, still seeking Jennifer or Travis, and found Sylvia collapsed on the sofa. If Fran saw the dead woman and heard Buddy barking outside, her immediate impulse was to find the dog and Jennifer. She didn't find Jennifer. The yips led her to the staircase. When she loosened the leash from the railing, Buddy jerked free. Fran chased him and ended up in the pond.

At the moment, I saw no danger to Fran from the death in the library. Even though she and Jennifer and Travis came and went on the Chandler terrace tonight, all apparently arrived and departed without attracting any notice.

I sniffed. No coal smoke.

Often I'd been distressed that the Rescue Express was coming to whisk me away when I felt I still had much to accomplish. Tonight the still clear air worried me. I'd left Fran safely in her bungalow, washing away the chill and scum of the pond. Surely her rescue was all that was required. Perhaps Wiggins was distracted by other worries. Perhaps he was dispatching an emissary to guide a plane safely through fog or reminding a mother to check the backyard in time to forestall a tragedy in the pool or nudging a young woman to call a young man, smooth over a misunderstanding. Wiggins has a great sympathy for lovers. He treasures those moments when an emissary links hands and hearts.

Yet I was puzzled that no coal smoke swirled. Surely all was well with Fran. Perhaps I would find a way for her to be happy again. I pondered that thought, remembered her unguarded face that revealed sadness and grief. Perhaps my focus tonight on this house of death was far afield from my purpose.

My uncertainty almost prompted an instant return to Fran's bungalow, but my second-grade teacher gently taught me to finish one task before beginning another. Fran was scared and her fear was linked to this house. I had a clear sense of how the investigation was proceeding in the library. What was happening outside?

Acting Chief Howie Harris stood with arms akimbo at the edge of the terrace. 'Fan out from the stairs. Take those Maglites and scour—'

I wondered what TV script prompted Howie's word choice. Honestly, have you ever heard anyone, police or civilian, instruct searchers to *scour* an area?

'—every square inch. We will find evidence of an intruder. Yeah,' he bellowed, 'scour the hillside. Fan out. Get out in the grass. A murderer fleeing the scene doesn't tippy-toe down well-lighted steps like a debutante leaving a party. That open door means somebody came out this way. Put those lights close to the ground.'

Maglites now illuminated the entire terrace. The bright red door at the end of the west wing was closed. A yellow door in the center of the central block of the house was also firmly shut. Likely the yellow door led into the kitchen. The green door at the end of the east wing remained wide open. I liked the painted doors. How easy to be specific. No need to say east wing or kitchen or west wing. 'Let's meet at the red door.' But now crime tape was draped across the green door and the library would always be remembered as the murder room.

Harris watched bobbing lights on the hillside below. 'It rained yesterday. The ground's still muddy—'

'Hey, Chief.' A high shout. 'Come look.' A Maglite swung in an arc, back and forth.

I reached a spot midway down the hill. The light exposed

several deep imprints in muddy soil. Time warps even the best shoes. The right sole was distinctive, a crease with a squiggly curve across the upper portion.

A Tiffany lamp glowed in Fran's small living room. All was silent, the silence of deep night. I slipped through the house, not to be intrusive but to get a sense of its layout. One room was quite dark except for a slant of moonlight across a portion of a bed and a chaise longue. A robe was draped over the chaise longue. My eyes adjusted to the dark. There was a form beneath covers. Muff lay at the foot of the bed. She lifted her head to look at me.

In the hallway I went straight to the bathroom. I eased the door shut, turned on the light. Damp clothes including bunched argyle socks lay in a pile near the bathtub. No boots. I scanned every inch of the bathroom, even opened cabinets. No boots.

I turned out the light and opened the door. Perhaps I moved too fast. I stepped into the foyer, came up hard against the protruding edge of a bench. 'Ouch.' I clapped my hands over my mouth, held my breath. The door to her bedroom remained closed with no telltale line of light beneath the door.

Limping a bit, I moved cautiously to the living room, flicked a switch. The bronze wheel lighting fixture on the ceiling offered soft warm illumination. I carefully paced the room, searching. No boots. I turned out the light, remembered the layout and advanced carefully to a swinging door. I stepped through, found the light switch.

My relief was euphoric when I saw the gray boots, freshly polished with no trace of mud, standing on a newspaper atop the tiled counter next to the sink.

I picked up the right boot. The leather was still moist, suggesting repeated applications of polish, likely in an effort to prevent cracking. I turned the boot over, saw the worn upper sole and the squiggly blemish so evident in the prints on the muddy hillside.

'Aunt Hortense?' Fran's voice was uneven, breathless.

I whirled. Of course the boot whirled as well, apparently hanging in mid-air with no signs of support.

Fran looked young and vulnerable in a short pink cotton

nightie, but she held a .22 pistol in her right hand. The gun was aimed straight at me. Yes, I know. I'm dead and I don't have to worry about following that trail again, but I do feel pain, witness my sore knee from cracking into the foyer bench.

I spoke with urgency. 'Do not shoot. I'm here to help.'

'You aren't Aunt Hortense?' There was a mixture of relief and uneasiness in her voice.

'Bailey Ruth Raeburn. Late of Adelaide, Oklahoma.' I don't usually chatter but the barrel was still aimed at me. 'Before your time. Our cruiser went down in the Gulf in 1978. I might have known your parents. If they lived in Adelaide.' I took two steps to the side. The boot moved also. 'But I don't know your last name.'

'Why is my boot floating?'

'I'm holding it.'

'Your voice.' An exclamation. 'I've heard you. Tonight. You helped me out of the pond.' Slowly the gun lowered. Her other hand reached up to smooth a tangle of golden curls. Her light blonde hair with its natural curl was much more attractive now than when plastered to her head after her dousing in the pond.

The gun now pointed at the kitchen floor. Whew. 'It was my pleasure.'

'You bumped into me at the edge of the woods. You were in my car.' She shivered. 'Aunt Hortense believed in ghoulies and ghosties and things that go bump in the night. I was always nice about it but I thought she was nuts. Look, my boot floating in the air makes me feel dizzy. Please put my boot down.'

I returned the boot to its mate.

'Aunt Hortense said someday she'd show me. She didn't say it nicely. Tonight's been hellish. Did she send you?'

I'd hoped that I might complete this mission and not Appear a single time. But the Precepts approve Appearing to reassure a frightened creature, and Fran surely had endured enough stress tonight.

I Appeared, colors swirling, happy colors, cream and rose and pale blue and a Heavenly orange. I felt stylish in a pale jade shaker-stitch roll-neck sweater and white wool trousers and white loafers with a jaunty jade bow that matched the sweater. I fluffed my red curls, smiled.

She didn't smile. Instead, she sagged against the door jamb. 'I've lost my mind.' She spoke in a monotone. 'Somebody shoved me up on the dock. I heard a voice at the edge of the woods. Now I'm imagining my boot hanging in the air and a redhead in my kitchen.'

I was eager to help. 'Could I fix you a nice hot toddy?'

Fran looked at me with an odd smile.

To my relief, the gun still pointed at the floor.

'Sure. Why not? All visiting ghosts know how to make hot toddies. That or my nutty mind is looking for comfort. But sure, I'll get the brandy.'

When she'd retrieved the ingredients, placed them on the counter a space away from the boots on the newspaper, I patted her shoulder, ignored her flinch, and said happily, 'I'm famous for my hot toddies.' Famous might be an exaggeration but Bobby Mac always said they were swell. I measured the brandy and lemon juice and honey and added boiling water and poured the fragrant mixture into two cheerful red-dotted ceramic mugs that Fran provided.

She kept up a running commentary. 'Just standing here watching. Big dollop of honey. A little more than I add but hey you have to allow a visiting ghost a free hand.' She held out her hands, looked at them. 'There they are. Not at the counter. Not pouring. Not stirring. But presto, there are the toddies. What fun.' She didn't sound like a woman having a grand time.

I beamed at her. 'The toddy will cheer you up.'

She glanced at the clock. 'Almost one a.m. Perhaps I'm into a new lifestyle. To bed at eleven. Can't sleep. Finally drift off. Then I hear noises and get up and imagine a ghost who makes hot toddies. But I didn't make them. This bright redhead made them. But hey, it's all my imagination.'

We settled in the living room. Fran dropped into an easy chair. She placed the gun on a side table. I handed her the toddy. She took the mug, stared at it, then slowly lifted her head to regard me. I was opposite her on a small sofa. I took a long slow sip. Bobby Mac always said a woman who could make a good hot toddy was a jewel beyond price. I murmured with satisfaction, 'Jewel beyond price.'

Fran carefully placed her mug on a malachite-topped side table. 'I don't have any jewels. But you know what, I'd like to have an amethyst necklace, blue as the sky, big chunks of amethyst. Since I can imagine a redhead in a gorgeous sweater and voices and floating boots, why not jewels?' There was the slightest quiver of hysteria in her voice.

The brandy infused me with warmth, but my muscles sagged with fatigue. I wanted to finish the toddy and find a bed. 'Do you have a guest bedroom?'

'Jewels, no. Spare bed, yes. You're welcome to snuggle in. Let's finish our toddies and call it a night.' She drank half the toddy.

I took another sip. I spoke conversationally. 'After you found Sylvia Chandler dead on the sofa—'

Her eyes widened and her face sagged.

'—you rushed outside. You heard Buddy yipping. But when you untied his leash from the railing, he got away. You ran after him.'

'Down the hill.' Her eyes held a memory of darkness and panic and a skidding descent.

'You left footprints.'

The words hung between us like a carcass strung on a pole.

Fran put down her mug, stared at me as if I were a combination of a witch doctor and a boa constrictor.

'So,' I was cheerful, 'the first thing to do is get rid of the boots. I'll take them to the lake and weight them with rocks. No one will ever see them again.'

She jumped to her feet.

I was right behind her as she rushed into the kitchen, grabbed the leather boots from the counter. She whirled, clutching the boots tight to her chest, and pushed past me with only a single frozen moment when her arm brushed against me.

I chased after her as she hurried through the living room. 'Fran, we have to talk.' How many dramas have heard those words uttered in despair or hope or anger or command?

As she opened her bedroom door, I gripped her arm.

She shuddered, pulled free, the boots firmly clasped to her body. 'I'm going to bed. If I have to endure a nightmare, it's more comfortable under the covers.' The door slammed in my face, a lock clicked.

Of course locks are no barrier to me. But Fran was in no mood for reasonable conversation. Tomorrow would do. I called out, 'Good night, sleep tight,' in hopes of calming her. I heard a thump or two beyond the door but no cheery response. I knew I was at the moment unwelcome. I needed to pep her up. I'd get up early and fix a delicious breakfast.

In the kitchen, I checked the refrigerator, spotted everything I would need. I am tidy. I retrieved the mugs from the living room, rinsed hers, gave my almost full mug a regretful look, poured out the contents, held the mug under the faucet. Before I sought refuge in the guest bedroom, I had one more task.

I found Fran's purse on a table in the foyer. I pulled out her billfold, studied her driver's license: Frances Mitchell Loring, 503 Minerva Street, b. 6 July 1988. The purse held the usual contents, blush, eyeliner, a compact, comb, a set of keys, a silver cardcase. I opened the case. The script was ornate: Mitchell Antiques, 206 Main Street, Adelaide, Oklahoma 74820. Frances Mitchell Loring, Prop. 508-ANT-IQUE A legend in gold letters at the bottom of the card: Find Your Treasure at Mitchell Antiques. A small leather folder held three photographs. Fran in a summery dress stood with her arms wide in welcome in front of a plate-glass window. Ornate gold letters proclaimed: Mitchell Antiques. Fran was quite lovely and young in the second photo. She glowed with happiness in a simply styled ivory wedding dress. A tall, slightly stooped man in a tuxedo gazed down at her, his face equally joyful. The third photo was a testament to summer and to love. Hand in hand, they splashed through shallow water at the seashore, laughing, happy, living in the moment. He was possibly ten or fifteen years older than Fran. I liked his face, intelligent, thoughtful, eager; a man who listened when others spoke.

I carried that glow with me as I settled in for the night in the spare bedroom. I chose pale blue flannel pajamas. As I smoothed a sleeve, I added silvery seashells and admired the adorable pattern. Seashells are magical, a connection to tide and sand. I slept fitfully as muddy gray boots marched past a

reviewing stand where I shivered in a sharp wind. Thump.
Thump. Thump. I watched boots bigger than boxcars halt,
stamp, swing about, thump, thump, thump.

I sat bolt upright, realized the top cover had slipped to the
floor. I shivered, blinked away sleep, saw the hands of
the bedside clock. Seven a.m.

Thump. Thump. Thump.

I disappeared, changing into a luxuriously soft and warm
azure-blue cotton top with embroidery at the front and cuffed
long sleeves. Gray flannel slacks and thick wool socks in
fleece-lined ankle boots provided more warmth. I fluffed my
hair as I reached the front door. I might be invisible but I am
not careless in my appearance.

Thump. Thump. Thump. A male voice was loud, brusque.
'Police. Open up.'

Fran was breathing fast as she reached the foyer.

The demand came again. 'Police. Open up.'

Her hand shook as she gripped the doorknob. Her left arm
was bent as she tried to pull on a navy-blue wool robe with
red piping at the wrists and hem. Her curly blonde ringlets
were sleep tousled. She was barefoot.

Thump. Thump. Thump. 'Po—'

Fran turned on the porch light and pulled the door open.
Cold air swept inside. She stared at the two figures facing
her, each holding out a leather folder open to display
identification.

I knew them, in the past would have welcomed their presence. Detective Judy Weitz's rather worn blue-and-green plaid
winter coat had a frayed cuff. Plain black would have been
more flattering. I winced at the purple scarf. A few wisps of
soft brown hair edged free of the silk. Her face was expres-
sionless, but her blue eyes were alert and wary. She'd seen
too much darkness, domestic violence, robbery victims with
injuries, overdosed teenagers, abused children, to approach the
world unguardedly. Don Smith's handsome face had lines of
fatigue, but he looked especially masculine and athletic in a
leather aviator jacket, dark slacks, and cordovan loafers. He
carried a small square black plastic case in his left hand.

'Judy.' Fran's voice had a wondering tone.

Judy took a deep breath. 'Detective Weitz. We have a search warrant.' She opened her shoulder bag, drew out a document with the seal of the county judge, held the stiff papers out.

Fran slowly lifted her hand, took the document, didn't look at it. 'I was going to call you today. I found the cameo you were looking for. Maybe you won't want it now.' Fran stood straight, head up, shoulders back. She waved her hand with the official document. 'Look wherever you want.'

My immediate instinct was to pop ahead to Fran's bedroom, find the boots. But I couldn't make them invisible.

Judy gave Don a quick glance.

There was a flash of sympathy in his eyes. He took over. 'Mrs Loring, please accompany us.'

Fran watched silently as Don and Judy methodically searched the foyer and its closet. In the living room, they lifted every cushion, moved furniture, slid out every drawer. The bathroom cabinets were opened and again every drawer examined.

I waited near the foot of Fran's bed, a queen size with old-fashioned brass headstand.

Don stepped inside, paused. His face reflected in turn surprise then an odd flash of sadness. As he walked toward the bed, his footsteps sounded heavy. Judy followed, her face determinedly blank.

Fran watched from the doorway, looking small and defenseless in her navy-blue robe.

The bed was rumpled, obviously its occupant had departed in haste, a quilt flung back, a pillow askew.

The detectives stared at the pair of leather boots nestled next to the unused pillow.

Don raised a dark eyebrow. 'Do you usually sleep with boots, Mrs Loring?'

Fran stood stiff and still, made no answer. Her shoulders were back, but her lips trembled. She looked despairing, hopeless.

Judy slipped her phone from a side pocket, filmed the boots, the bed, the remainder of the room.

In the doorway, Fran gripped the doorjamb on either side.

Don handed the square case to Judy. She placed the case

on the bed, snapped the lock, lifted the lid. She plucked out plastic gloves, pulled them on. She walked to the head of the bed, used a pincer to grip the right boot.

In the doorway, Fran pleaded, 'Don't take my boot.' It was as if she cried for a piece of herself. There was no hint of fear, simply anguish at the loss of the boot.

Don studied her face, staring eyes and sunken cheeks, lips parted and quivering. Face creased in a frown, he looked toward the bed as the right gray boot was seized, back at Fran.

Tears slipped down Fran's cheeks unchecked. She was oblivious to his regard. Her whole being was focused on the boot sliding into a large clear plastic bag. Her hands dropped. She took a step toward the bed.

Judy picked up a white square. She carefully printed date, time, location, and description of boot taken into evidence. She creased the back, pulled off the protective covering, pressed the adhesive surface to the bag.

Fran pressed a balled fist against her lips.

Judy plucked another clear plastic bag from the case, reached out with the pincers.

Fran shuddered as if she stared into an abyss.

Don watched her, his gaze puzzled.

I understood his reaction. He and Judy came seeking boots to match prints on the muddy hillside behind the Chandler house. He would have expected Fran to look frightened or stone-faced or defiant or sunnily innocent. Instead, she wept. She wept and turned to look at a mahogany table centered along the wall opposite the bed.

He looked, too.

On the wall above the table was a man's portrait.

I recognized the man who stood next to Fran in her wedding gown. He was younger in the wedding photo, perhaps late thirties to her early twenties. He was older in the bedroom portrait, dark hair flecked with silver, an inviting, genial face, firm featured but with an air of civility and engagement, intelligent blue eyes, a quizzical half-smile.

Don looked from the portrait to the table-top. A pair of men's soft doeskin gloves lay next to a well-worn copy of *A Tale of Two Cities*. Below the portrait was a chess set, ivory pieces in place ready for the opening move. On one corner was a green ceramic bowl with seashells piled high. Lining the back of the table were assorted cards, birthday, Christmas, Valentine, St Patrick. A stack of letters filled one corner.

Don walked toward the table.

'No.' Her cry was deep, painful.

He looked at her. 'We got what we came for.' He nodded at the table. 'I minored in history. I had three classes from Professor Loring. Best professor I ever had.'

Fran turned her hands out in supplication. 'The boots, please. He gave them to me.'

Judy Weitz's eyes were bright with unshed tears, but she spoke briskly. 'I will add a directive that the owner requests the return of the contents in the event the material is not needed for a trial.'

FOUR

I perched on the edge of the back seat.

Judy Weitz drove with her eyes on the road and her hands clamped on the wheel. 'Sometimes I don't like my job very much.' Her usually crisp tone was forlorn.

Don slouched in the passenger seat, long legs outstretched. 'Yeah.'

She turned at the end of the block. 'Two blocks down, then to the right?'

'Yeah. Third house on the north side.'

'The tape was running when I got to the station this morning. First thing I saw when I got to my desk. Subject filmed by security camera at far edge of the Chandler terrace at eight twenty-two p.m. My job to get posters printed, pix to show around town. But I knew who she was. I've shopped at her store for years.' Another turn. 'I didn't have a choice.'

'Yeah.' His dark brows knitted in a frown.

Judy shot him a quick glance. 'You were up most of the night?'

He rubbed a bristly cheek. 'I spent a lot of time on FB. Who cares if you made chili last night? Or hung your ass over the railing at Niagara? Or came *this* close to the winning lottery ticket? People put the damnedest things on their FB pages. Plus I got DMV info and bios from company websites. I have a real nice dossier on all the people in the Chandler house last night. I sent the dossiers to Acting Chief of Police Howie Harris. He about fainted that I'd worked most of the night. Squeaked he'd promised the mayor: No Overtime. I'm to stay home today and I get paid like I worked regular days instead of overtime. He's gone nuts paring down hours since Sam's been gone.'

The car slowed and turned into a drive.

He grabbed the door handle.

The redwood house was strikingly beautiful in the early

morning sunlight, a house that promised unusual vistas, refreshment for weary souls.

He opened the door, swung out. 'Howie said I should have asked him. Asked what? Papa, can I go pee? I'm a detective. You got a murder. You got six people on site, not counting a sick man and his attendant. Any one of the six could have killed the woman. It is, double-duh, called opportunity. Oh no, says Inspector Clouseau, the killer came from outside. How do we know the murderer came from the outside? Because,' Don's voice was heavy with sarcasm, 'the back door to the east wing was open. Could someone in the house have staged it that way? How could I make such a suggestion?' Don's tone was savage. 'Howie squealed that these people are rich and the mayor yada-yada-yada.' Don looked at the two evidence bags in the back seat. 'And now he's got her boots. But that's OK. She's not rich.'

Sam Cobb's second-floor office in the police station was dim and quiet with that lonely feeling of an unoccupied room. I'd spent time in his office both seen and unseen. I opened the blinds to thin November sunlight, turned on his desk lamp, settled in his chair. The chair was chilly and the desktop bare and dusty.

Much was unchanged, his old brown leather sofa that faced the windows, the detailed maps of Adelaide on the walls, the old-fashioned blackboard with real chalk in the tray. Almost automatically my left hand dropped and pulled out the lower drawer. I retrieved a half-full bag of M&Ms, poured out a handful, replaced the bag in the bottom drawer. The sweet crunchy candies gave me a spurt of energy.

I hoped Sam hadn't been gone long. I was counting on taking advantage of his disdain for the mayor's password policy. She insisted all city employees change the password weekly. Sam, looking like Broderick Crawford staring down a pompous sheriff, said passwords gave him the willies and if his desk wasn't safe, nothing was safe, so he kept his list of passwords in his center drawer. I opened the drawer, found a list of words scrawled in over-large masculine handwriting: Truman, termites, tomahawk, tiddlywinks, tease, traffic. The first three were checked off. I turned to the computer monitor, typed tiddlywinks.

'Sam, I love you, you great big dependable stubborn man.'

I looked at his e-mails. Bingo. The most recent e-mail was this morning. To: Sam Cobb. From: Don Smith. I clicked.

The first paragraph was a zinger:

> Hi Sam,
>
> AC Howie Harris is following current protocol re. investigation into last night's homicide of Sylvia Chandler, second wife of Arthur Chandler, at the Chandler mansion: Limited use of manpower, deference to residents of the home based on conclusion murder committed by an intruder since a back door to the terrace was open. The attached file for your records as contents deemed superfluous by AC.
>
> Thinking of you and Claire and hoping all is going as well as possible.
>
> Don

I clicked on the attachment, smothered a soft whoop as I read succinct dossiers of every person present in Chandler House last night including the victim. I never excelled at memorization. Bobby Mac could reel off Gunga Din or Dickens quotes while I had trouble remembering a grocery list, which was why I made grocery lists even though I often couldn't find them.

Down the hall I found the supply room with the printer which served the entire department. I gave myself a thumbs-up that I'd arrived at the station before the eight a.m. shift. The new budget likely didn't provide for more than a couple of officers on duty overnight.

I returned to Sam's office, clicked Print, then closed the file, clicked out of e-mail. I was in high good humor when I returned to the supply room. The last sheet was sliding out of the printer. I picked up the sheets.

Of course I wasn't visible.

The sheets were visible.

'Hazel?' The voice behind me sounded choked.

I whirled toward the door.

AC Howie Harris gazed frantically around the room. 'Hazel, where are you? Hazel, papers are floating.'

Clutching the sheaf of papers, I ducked down behind the printer out of Howie's field of vision.

One slow footstep after another came nearer and nearer.

'Drat,' I clapped my free hand over my mouth.

The footsteps stopped. 'Hazel, where are you?'

Hazel was likely driving too fast to squeal into the parking lot at City Hall and fly toward the building.

I and my precious sheets were backed into a corner between the big printer and a wall.

The footsteps resumed, were very near. When Howie came around the end of the printer he would see the sheets aloft. At this point each sheet looked billboard-sized to me. The sheets were a physical reality and required transport through space. No thinking *Sam's office* and arriving there instantly.

There was nothing else for it. I rose to the ceiling and zoomed out into the hall, the papers apparently self-propelled just below the ceiling.

Running steps followed. 'Hazel!'

I got to Sam's door before Howie rounded the corner. I turned the knob, stepped inside, yanked the door shut. I ran across the room, opened the M&M drawer, picked up the sack, poured out a handful, slapped the sheets into the drawer, closed it.

Perhaps Howie heard Sam's door open and close. Whatever, a breathless Howie burst into Sam's office, his watery blue eyes scanning the ceiling in search of airborne printer sheets.

Howie shut the door behind him. His blue eyes brightened as they surveyed the room. His breathing slowed as the office appeared calm and empty with no vagrant sheets of paper sailing through the air. A minute passed, another. He gazed about with a proprietorial air, then strode, chest out, to the blackboard. He picked up the chalk, printed in all caps:

CHIEF OF POLICE HOWIE HARRIS.

His back was to me but I saw the strut of his shoulders, a man envisioning his future. He turned, gazed at Sam's bare desk. 'Eat your heart out, Sammie. Neva—'

I poured a handful of M&Ms, popped them into my mouth, glared toward the blackboard. The mayor would love to replace Sam with Howie, but were Howie and the mayor now on a first-name basis?

'—called me early this morning, said I was just the man for the job, I'd already saved the department eight thousand four hundred and thirty-three dollars. And I'm just getting started.' He walked toward the desk, shoulders back.

I eased the left lower drawer open, returned the candies, closed the drawer.

He stopped a foot away as the sound of a closing drawer registered. He edged close to the desk, moved around the side, peered at the drawers, all innocently shut. A pause and his hand touched the side of Sam's chair, tugged. Of course the chair was occupied. By me. The chair hardly budged.

He frowned, gave a yank just as I stood up.

The chair rolled sideways and tipped to the floor. Howie bumped against the desk, grabbed at a corner for support.

I walked to the blackboard, picked up the eraser, swiped, slapped the eraser into the tray so forcefully that chalk dust rose.

Still off balance, he jerked to look at the blackboard. A wisp of dust lingered above the tray, the board was smeared and Chief Howie Harris was no more. His eyes looked like knobs on a baton.

I was at the door. I yanked the door wide open.

Crabs scuttle. Earthworms scoot. Turkeys flap. Howie's exit was a delicious blend of all three. Running steps faded in the distance.

I slammed the door shut, punched the lock for good measure, then leaned against the door and laughed. It isn't easy to do but I laughed and munched sweet M&Ms at the same time, a Heavenly—

Steel wheels clacked on silver rails. Coal smoke swirled. Whooo. Whooo.

I stood at attention.

'Bailey Ruth.' Wiggins's deep voice was stern. 'Precept Five.'

I wished I dared suggest he Appear. In his station, he exudes warmth and kindness and understanding. I pictured him, stiff blue cap with a black bill atop thick reddish hair, a florid face with laughter lines, sideburns and handlebar mustache, perfectly ironed starched white cotton shirt with garters on his upper arms, heavy gray wool trousers held up by both suspenders and a large black belt with a silver buckle. He didn't sound nearly so formidable in person. 'Oh, Bailey Ruth.' Deep disappointment.

I rushed to claim some high ground. 'I didn't Appear, not once, when I saved Fran and Buddy from the pond or during Jennifer's outrageous claim she and Buddy were in her bedroom all evening or riding in Fran's car or at the Chandler house, not until Fran caught me in her kitchen with her boots.' I quickly recited Precepts Three and Four. 'I followed Precept Three: Work behind the scenes without making your presence known, and Precept Four: Become visible only when absolutely necessary.'

He didn't relent. 'Precept Five.'

I recited with a sigh. 'Precept Five: Do not succumb to the temptation to confound those who seem to oppose you.'

Silence.

'Wiggins, I can explain. Please join me on Sam's sofa.' I Appeared in a high-necked white cotton long-sleeve blouse buttoned at the throat, plain straight navy-blue skirt, ankle length, and demure navy slippers. Think 1910 school marm. I sat quite straight, my hands gracefully folded in my lap, the picture of decorum.

In a moment the sofa beside me creaked. As he Appeared, sunlight streaming into the office made his russet hair bright and his stiff white shirt gleam. But I didn't see his wide mouth stretch in a smile. He was grave. 'Emissaries have a special duty to avoid disturbing earthly creatures, especially those who lack confidence.'

'Lack confidence?' I was off and running. 'Howie Harris is a weasel and not very smart and he's cutting corners in an investigation because pleasing the mayor matters more to him than actually finding out what happened and he treats rich people like they're special and he'll fasten on Fran Loring like algae on a pond because she's not rich and she was outside and he's decided an open door means the killer came from outside. Detective Smith—'

'Detective Smith' – Wiggins's tone was approving. One big broad hand brushed a piece of lint from the right knee of his gray flannel trousers – 'is trying to do things right. He's looking into the people who were at the house last night because any one of them could have killed Sylvia Chandler but he can't work overtime so he's home twiddling his thumbs today or maybe having a bloody Mary he's so disgusted.'

'Detective Smith will do the right thing.' A pause. 'Precept Five.'

We were back to people not doing the right thing, i.e., me.

'I am distressed by your actions.' His gaze was sorrowful. 'An emissary from the Department of Good Intentions must never diminish anyone.'

Coal smoke intensified, swirled around me, obscuring the sun spilling through the windows.

Bobby Mac once told me that when a redhead gets an idea in mind, she clings to it like a barnacle to a pier. I took it as a compliment. I wasn't giving up. 'Howie Harris is trying to sabotage Sam Cobb. Howie wants to be chief, not acting chief. Howie doesn't care a fig about Sam and how hard he works and what a good job he does.'

Wiggins said gently, 'Howie's parents abandoned him. An elderly aunt raised him. He never did anything quite well enough. When he tried out for a play and wasn't chosen, his aunt told him, "You have your father's weak chin. Too bad."'

I wasn't feeling charitable. 'That was then. This is now. He's going to arrest Fran Loring.'

'That won't happen.' Wiggins spoke with utter confidence. The coal smoke thinned.

I was stunned. 'Why not?'

'Despite flouting several Precepts, I've decided your mission will continue. With you present,' there was a slight rumble of laughter, Wiggins loved a good pun, 'you will see her through her current travail.'

I snapped my fingers, noticed their color and changed the polish from flamingo to a subdued pink. 'Just like that, I suppose.'

'Bailey Ruth,' he sounded as though he was about to bestow a medal or perhaps hang a wreath of roses around my neck, 'you always triumph.'

I flung out my hand. I didn't feel at all pink. I changed my nails to deep purple. I felt like Tallulah Bankhead on a tear. 'That's because I kept track of investigations on Sam's computer. Howie Harris isn't going to send Sam a blow-by-blow of his pared-down investigation.'

'Sam became quite comfortable visiting with you.' A pause. 'In person. Often at Lulu's Café.'

Wiggins was reminding me of my flagrant disregard of Precept Four: Become visible only when absolutely necessary. Wiggins no doubt knew each and every time I was visible to Sam, including an occasional early meeting at Lulu's Café with an attendant delicious breakfast. Breakfast. Part of a hot toddy and a few fistfuls of M&Ms were my most recent repast. I was famished.

'Now,' he stood, started to fade, 'go have a good breakfast at Lulu's and figure out what happened. You can do it. I know you will.' His voice was growing fainter. 'But that's not your most important task, of course. Don and—'

He was gone.

Don and . . .?

I strive to be an ever-obedient emissary. Do not guffaw, please.

I thought *Don and . . .* I remained firmly in Sam's office. I thought *Don's car.*

I stood beside the gorgeous muscle car in a parking lot at White Deer Park, Adelaide's lovely municipal park with a lake and carousel and an amphitheater. The car enchanted me. I touched a fender of the low-slung, meticulously maintained, fire-engine-red Corvette. Bobby Mac and our son Rob would salivate at the prospect of a ride. I pictured them, dark-haired Bobby Mac and carrot-topped Rob hanging out the windows like eager Labs. I sat in the driver's seat. OK. I'm a car hound, too. I once had a tan Beetle and always felt jaunty when I drove her. The Corvette's black leather upholstery was luxurious. I put my hands on the sleek wheel, gazed through the windshield.

Don leaned against the railing at the end of the pier. The breeze off the lake ruffled his dark hair. He looked out at the water at two elegant swans. He reached into a plastic bag and pulled out a handful of shredded lettuce that he tossed on the water. The swans glided near to gobble their treat, turned, swam away.

He balled up the bag, stuffed it in a side pocket of his leather jacket, then looked at his wristwatch and walked toward shore. As he came close I noticed that he looked thoughtful, but there was no trace of worry or concern. He obviously was in no need of my oversight. I would follow Wiggins's instructions, enjoy breakfast at Lulu's and ponder Wiggins's parting injunction that my most important task was *Don and . . .*

Don reached the edge of the parking lot. I lingered for a moment, entranced by an unusual miniature hanging from the rear-view mirror, a tiny, beautifully carved redwood house. I smiled in recognition. The charm was a small replica of Don's house, gorgeous redwood with a broad porch and big windows to welcome sunlight, a house designed with imagination and vision.

As the driver's door swung out, I flowed to the pavement. I watched the Corvette zoom away. Wiggins made *Don and . . .* my special charge. I was intrigued by the detective's choice of a home and the car he drove. The car reflected a love of speed and admiration for a superb machine. The house indicated a free spirit in architecture that soared. I once had a good friend who was a reporter on the *Gazette* and she told me, 'Everybody has a story. You just have to listen.' I wondered if I would someday know Don Smith's story.

Lulu's Café is jam-packed from the opening whiff of Ozark bacon at six a.m. to the last bite of cherry pie at nine p.m. Wiggins was right. Sam Cobb and I often met at Lulu's, a favorite haunt (irresistible) of the Adelaide police department. I smoothed the sleeve of my purple pullover, a spectacular enhancement for white wool slacks. Purple ankle boots matched my polish. A white scarf added dash. I stood just inside the door and surveyed the room. Several uniformed officers occupied the third booth. There was no trace of

Detective Don Smith. I concluded I was led to Lulu's to enjoy a peaceful and energizing breakfast while I mulled what I knew and mapped out a campaign to protect Fran Loring.

'Excuse me.' The booming voice was a demand to step out of the way. I was quick to turn, redheads do not suffer rudeness gladly, then swung away, lifting the scarf to hide the lower portion of my face.

Mayor Neva Lumpkin, her hair an improbable gold, sailed past. AC Howie Harris, natty in a red-and-white checked shirt and gray trousers, hurried to catch up.

I knew my duty. I stepped outside, gave a quick glance up and down the street. A few pedestrians moved along the sidewalk, all with downturned faces staring at cell phones. I disappeared. In an instant I was perched next to Howie Harris and opposite the mayor in a red leatherette booth. They ordered: French toast with whipped cream and maraschino cherries, a Lulu special, for the mayor; a he-man breakfast for Howie – steak, sausage, hash browns, scrambled eggs, and biscuits with cream gravy.

'Bring me up to date,' the mayor ordered. A large woman, she was a bit wedged between the table-top and the back of the booth. She was not a woman for casual dress. Her navy-blue wool suit was nicely cut. A triple-strand pearl necklace was perhaps a tad overdone.

Howie rushed to speak. 'I avoided overtime by comping last night's techs with two days off. Ditto the patrol officers and Detective Smith.' A slight frown. 'Smith took it on himself to interview the residents of the house. I told him the perp came from outside. He said he was just following protocol on a homicide. I told him we have a new protocol. No unnecessary reports. And,' Howie was jubilant, 'my initial assessment – an outside perp – was confirmed. A security camera is in place on each side of the terrace to film any trespasser. The cameras are mounted below the gutters on the outer walls of each wing. The angle of the cameras is set to film any movement at the edges of the terrace. The major portion of the terrace and the steps to the lower garden aren't filmed. It's designed to record trespassers from either side.'

'Of course,' the mayor trumpeted approval, 'the main part

of the terrace isn't filmed. The Chandlers often hosted barbecues on the terrace. It would be offensive to guests if security cameras were trained on them. This is a testament to the Chandlers' graciousness. They wouldn't dream of filming guests.' The mayor appeared almost overwhelmed by this evidence of gentility. 'They would never wish to violate the privacy of their guests.'

And so, I thought grimly, Fran Loring was filmed, but not Jennifer Roberts. That also told me that Travis came up and left by the stairs to the terrace. He drove away from his house, parked midway up the block, took the path through the woods to the stairs. Since he lived at the foot of the hill, he would usually arrive via the stairs to the terrace.

Harris was quick to agree. 'The Chandlers are tops in this town, always have been. I'll make it clear to Smith they deserve every consideration.' Howie wanted the mayor to know that he understood their special status. 'I will make sure they are kept informed as to the progress of the investigation. I know they will be relieved that we are right on top of everything. This morning Detective Weitz identified the woman filmed by the security camera as Frances Loring. Last night the crime-scene techs found a woman's footprints midway down the hill behind the house, footprints obviously made by a fleeing figure. The forward portion of one print revealed a distinctive marking. Detectives Weitz and Smith served a search warrant on Loring this morning. They took into custody a pair of boots that reflected recent polish. The sole of the right boot matched the print on the hillside so that further confirms her presence behind the Chandler house last night.' If he'd spread out a full house and won a jackpot, Harris couldn't have been happier.

The mayor frowned. 'Loring. The one who owns Mitchell Antiques?'

He looked uneasy. 'Yes.'

The mayor's face was still for a moment. Likely she was calculating the net worth of Fran Loring vis-à-vis the Chandlers. No contest. 'Is Loring in custody?'

'Not yet. Loring likely figures we got the boots to match prints in the Chandler yard. The boots showed evidence of recent cleaning. Instead of bringing her in for questioning and all the overtime that would require, I decided to leave her hanging over the weekend. I've instructed an officer to visit the Chandler house this afternoon, a uniformed officer, much cheaper than a detective, and show the security footage to the residents, see if any of them know her or know of any quarrel she had with the victim. I'm going to let Loring wonder and worry. When are the police coming? What are they doing? What do they know? If she makes a break, tries to escape, that will clinch the case.' He fumbled in his hip pocket. 'I've got the clip here, Mayor. This will sink her with a jury.' He held out the phone.

I bent close to the mayor as she held the oblong in her plump fingers.

I drew in a quick breath. Fran was at the east edge of the terrace, staring forward, her thin, narrow face tense, eyes wide with alarm, lips pressed together. She was leaning forward as if listening.

Howie might have been showing off a prize catfish hauled from a lake. 'Yessireebob. The camera caught her full face. Looks like she's figuring out her next move. Did she sneak inside? Or did she have an appointment? Whatever, you can tell she's upset. My guess is Loring knew the woman spent most evenings in the library without locking the terrace door. Loring went in. Maybe she walked up to the fireplace, said it's cold outside, and maybe they had words or maybe she just grabbed the poker and slammed. I'm betting there's bad blood there. As soon as we find out why she hated Sylvia Chandler, we'll arrest her.'

Their plates arrived.

The mayor clapped her hands together in delight.

The skinny waitress quivered.

'Not you, dearie,' the mayor boomed. 'This man has done outstanding work. Stellar work. Put his meal on my ticket.'

Howie's blue eyes shone. Pink touched his plump cheeks. 'Mayor, I am honored.' He sat straighter as he basked in her approval.

I wasn't impressed. For sure she would put the meals on her office tab, a working breakfast. But the little boy who never pleased his stern aunt gloried in his moment in the sun.

* * *

Outside I checked the street before I Appeared. I was careful inside to keep my back to the mayor and Howie Harris. I slid on to a leatherette-topped stool at the far end of the counter. I welcomed the scent of coffee and bacon, Patsy Cline on the jukebox, animated conversations around me, men's voices deep, women's high and soft as the flutter of wings. I ordered a waffle with whipped cream and, of course, the cherries, sausage and grits, black coffee. The service at Lulu's is always quick. I ate fast, seeking sustenance, while my thoughts darted. Fran was safe from arrest until Monday. I wished for Wiggins's direction or Sam Cobb's wise counsel. I sniffed. No coal smoke. And Sam absent from Adelaide and no mention of his return. Sam loved the old cliché, 'Get the facts, ma'am'; he warned against missing the trees because of the forest. It was as if I saw a compass swing to true north. Everything was muddled about last night. *'Get the facts, ma'am.'*

I arrived unseen at Mitchell Antiques shop. The Open sign hung in the window. Inside I admired Sheffield silver, cameos, cut-glass pitchers and bowls, carved ivories, a blunderbuss on a plaque, Chinese porcelain, a Dresden shepherdess. My gaze lingered on a massive sea chest with faded travel stickers. Each item once belonged to a spirit long gone. Each had a history, could tell stories of love and loss, strife and golden hours, journeys and quiet days. Fran sat at a maple desk. Even in the shop's dim light the wood glowed. She held a pen loosely in one hand. A yellow legal pad lay on the desktop.

I looked over her shoulder. A single sentence.

Oh Bill, I need you.

FIVE

Fran lightly tapped each word – *Oh Bill, I need you.* – with the tip of the pen. Briefly she closed her eyes, then opened them, sat straight, chin lifted. 'Come on, Fran.' Her voice was stern. 'Do what Bill always told you to do. Put everything in order. Make a plan.' She picked up the pen, printed fast.

I went to dinner last night at Travis and Jennifer's. Travis was full of plans for the big art festival next summer. He told us Sylvia Chandler was going to make him the featured artist. We carried our coffee into the living room, Travis still talking nineteen to the dozen. And then he decided he wanted to tell Sylvia he'd just finished a new painting that would be perfect for the festival poster. He pulled out his cell, called her and launched into a description of the painting, said the dimensions were perfect for big posters. Then he broke off. I guess she interrupted, his face got all twisted in a frown. He hunched his shoulders, exploded, 'You told me I'd be featured. You can't do that to me. I've told people and I've got a painting for the poster—' Suddenly he held out the phone, stared at it, his face all jutty, the way he looks when he's furious. I knew she'd hung up on him. The back of his neck turned red. He jammed the phone in his pocket, started for the door. He was swearing. I ran after him, grabbed his arm. He pulled away. He was so mad I don't think he even saw me. He slammed the door. In a minute we heard the car roar. I asked Jennifer why she didn't do anything to stop him. She gave me an aren't-you-silly look, said, 'Oh you know Travis, he'll get it out of his system.' I kept pressing her, said she'd better go after him, go up to the Chandler house and see if she could smooth things over. Finally she gave a sigh and said, 'Oh all right, I'll take Buddy out and go up and see if he's there, remind Sylvia artists are artists.' She took Buddy and left. I thought Jennifer was probably going around the block and would come back and look vague and say everything was fine. I paced up and down for a few minutes and decided I had to do something. I hurried out to the street. Travis's car was parked halfway up the hill.

'Halfway up the hill? Why halfway up the hill?'

Fran stiffened. Her head slowly turned. Had I been visible, we would have been looking at each other. 'You're here.'

It is good that I'm not sensitive. She might have sounded equally thrilled if a tarantula was perched on her shoulder. I simply said, 'I need to know exactly what happened last night.'

'Hearing voices isn't considered healthy.' Her tone was flat. 'But I can't see you,' she spoke with more energy, 'and please keep it that way. No wiggly colors. Anyway, who cares if you're here. I have to get last night straight in my mind. If I tell you everything, maybe I won't hear you anymore.' She ended up sounding quite cheerful. 'OK. Halfway up the hill? Those woods belong to the Chandlers. It's quicker to take a path through the woods to stairs that lead up to the terrace than to go to the house and park in the drive and ring the bell.'

'He must have felt on close terms with Mrs Chandler to take the back way to see her.'

'As close as he could manage. She was a mover and shaker in the art world. He saw her as his ticket to fame and fortune.'

'So he came and went there often?'

'Always with a painting. Or to talk about a painting. I don't even know if he liked her personally. Travis isn't interested in people unless they can help his career.'

A young man. An attractive older woman. 'Was he having an affair with her?' Sam once told me there are two triggers for most murders. Sex. Or money.

'He took the back path for convenience. Not sex. Sylvia Chandler was devoted to Arthur. This is a small town. Never any gossip about Sylvia Chandler. Travis was looking out for his career. He's an ambitious artist. Insanely ambitious? Maybe. He's good. He knows he's good. He'd say he's a brilliant artist. Sylvia knew her art. Did you look around the library? She collected art. She wrote articles for *Art in America*. She was director of the Art League and chair of Adelaide's Summer Art Festival. Invitation only. Being a featured artist at the festival guarantees lots of sales and attention from dealers and everyone who matters in the regional art world.'

I seized on the salient point. 'He started off in a fury to confront her.'

'That's just Travis. It doesn't mean anything. He loses his temper. He shouts. Storms around. That's all. He wouldn't hurt anyone.' But her eyes held a dark burden of fear.

The treks up the hillside came into focus. An ambitious artist. The director of the festival taking away his starring role. Travis slamming out of the house to go and protest. His wife following, though without enthusiasm. Fran seeking both of them.

I wondered if Fran's desperate urgency to find Travis was prompted by fear that this time his anger was beyond control, this time he moved in a red haze of fury, this time he would attack his tormentor.

'Jennifer went after him because you pushed her. Why did you go after them?' I watched her carefully. Would she tell me the truth?

She started to speak, stopped, took a breath. 'Old habits are hard to break. My mom married his dad when Travis was four. Maybe we all spoiled him, excused any tantrums because he was so gifted. He was already drawing.' A little touch of awe in her voice. 'He drew a galloping horse when he was only four that was amazing. I still have it. We all did everything we could to smooth the path for him, always excusing his quick temper. Artistic nature, you know. It was like watching a flamingo grow up. Special. I've always known he fudges the truth to get what he wanted. Last night I was Fran to the rescue one more time.'

I felt she spoke the truth, but perhaps not the whole truth. That dark fear flickered in her eyes.

'I wanted to save him from ruining his future. Sylvia wasn't a good person to antagonize. I know a bit about Sylvia Chandler.' Fran's voice hardened. 'She always looked at the bottom line and to hell with any collateral damage. A better-known artist would be a bigger draw. If Travis didn't like it, that was his problem. That's who she was. I thought I'd catch Jennifer, maybe persuade her to apologize to Sylvia, smooth everything over, promise he'd do everything to support the festival. He would have agreed after he got over his madness because it's a fabulous festival.'

'So you reached Travis's car and started on the path that leads to the stairs. Why did you leave the path and go up the hill through the woods?' That decision brought her on to the terrace from the side and into the view of the security camera. Travis and Jennifer came up the steps and must have left by the steps.

She shivered. 'I was on the path when I heard someone running. It scared me. There was something wild about the sound.'

'Did you see anyone?'

'I veered off the path and got into the deep woods. Frankly, I was hiding behind a big shrub. Then there was a clatter on the stairs, fast, faster.'

'Do you think it was Travis?'

'I don't know.' The answer was slow. 'I didn't really think. I just heard someone running and I was frightened, so I crouched behind this big bush and then someone was running on the path toward the street. I almost turned back but the running steps worried me. The steps were loud. I was almost sure I heard a man running. A big man. Oh, I knew it might be Travis. Why would he run? I felt I had to go up to the terrace, make sure everything was all right. I stayed in the woods. The stairs are lighted and I didn't want to be seen. It was a terrible climb. So dark. Tree branches creaking in the wind. I kept feeling like I wasn't alone. And after I heard the man running, oh I think I was almost to the top of the hill, I heard someone else on the stairs, a quick patter of feet. That must have been Jennifer. I don't know how I forced myself to keep going. Then it was awfully quiet. I got to the terrace. I saw the open door in the east wing and the lights flooding across the terrace. I could see a yellow door into the main portion of the house. It was closed. I looked across the terrace but the other wing was mostly in dark shadow. I looked again at the wide-open door. That open door on a cold night seemed wrong. I took one step and another and then I was at the door. I looked inside. I didn't see anyone but I had a bad feeling.

Something was wrong and Travis had been here. I went inside. The room was cold. Quiet. I kept walking and I came even with the sofa. I saw her. I thought I was going to faint. I saw the poker lying on the hearth. Someone crushed the life out of her and Travis had been terribly angry. I knew I should call the police, but how could I explain why I was there? And I didn't know where Travis was or if he had seen Sylvia. I just couldn't force myself to call anyone. I scarcely knew what I was doing. I looked all around the room, but there was nothing out of place and no one there. Somehow I stumbled back out on to the terrace.'

I pictured what may have happened. Travis left his house in a fury, parked the car on the street, took the path through the woods to the stairs, climbed to the terrace. Meanwhile, Jennifer left the house with the dog. Almost certainly Travis entered the library to confront Sylvia. Either he killed her or found her body. Jennifer reached the steps. Fran started out after Jennifer and Travis. Running steps. Fran was frightened and darted into the woods. Likely Jennifer too was shocked and took cover. I was sure Travis ran away from the library and down the steps. Clearly Jennifer then went up to the terrace, tied Buddy to the railing. Likely she too entered the library, saw Sylvia's body, and hurriedly fled, abandoning Buddy. Then Fran arrived at the side of the terrace, stepped into the view of the security camera.

Fran clasped her hands tightly together. 'I was shivering on the terrace and I heard Buddy yipping. I found him tied to the railing by the stairs.'

'Think back to those running steps.'

'Heavy steps. A man running. It almost had to be Travis.' A reluctant admission. 'He's always run from trouble, let other people pick up the pieces. I think he found her body and rushed out. Maybe Jennifer saw him. She certainly would have heard a man running. She's always vague and says whatever but even she would have wondered what was going on. I imagine she crept across the terrace, reached the door, listened, didn't hear anything. She double-dared herself to go inside, take a look.'

'Double-dared?'

'My sister-in-law is vague but she gets sharp if anything

will affect her. She knew Travis stormed out to talk to Sylvia. She heard a man running. Travis's temper never bothered her. She gets this little gleam in her eyes and says, "I always tell him his pictures are the best in the whole world." She'll give a little laugh and says he agrees, so he's happy. She knew he was crazy mad. That open door would seem odd. Grown-ups don't play double-dare. It's Jennifer's mantra. I don't know how many times she's said, "I double-dared myself to . . ." Jennifer trills on and recounts some episode where she, Double-Dare Brave Jennifer, accomplishes a daunting task. Oh yes, Jennifer would go inside. She found the body. She must have flown out of that room and run wildly to the steps and skittered down and raced straight home. She probably realized halfway there that she'd left Buddy, but she'd decide somehow that would all work out. Never in a million years would she have gone back up the steps to get him. Knowing her she figured I was around somewhere and I'd hear him and Buddy would be fine. That's how she thinks. The universe runs on a benign schedule for her benefit. And she will never admit she was anywhere near the Chandler library last night.'

'She won't have a choice.' I was excited. 'When Travis and Jennifer tell the police they both found Sylvia dead, you'll be in the clear.'

'When llamas tap dance. When Climate Changers throw a party for Frackers. When the Sahara is carpeted with four-leaf clovers.'

I was confident. 'When the police arrest you, surely they will speak up.'

Fran shook her head. 'Travis will paint some shocking splash of red and purple, admire his work, start the next painting. Jennifer will visit across a screen, huge-eyed, delighting in her Double-Dare Presence and ask, "What's it like being in jail?"'

'But you're family.' Mama always told us kids, "Doesn't matter how cross you are with each other at home, out in the world, it's one for all and all for one. You hear me now."'

Fran's laugh was short and not amused. 'All families are dysfunctional, and I will be living proof. But dream on, Cheerful Voice. Anyway, you've overlooked one point.'

'And that is?'

'I'm positive Sylvia was dead when Travis and Jennifer arrived. I can't prove it, but Travis explodes and then the next thing you know it's an arm across your shoulders. Yes, he was angry but I don't believe, won't believe, he would ever hurt anyone.'

Her voice was thin and darkness in her eyes told me her insistence on his innocence reflected what she hoped was true, but that she wasn't in her heart absolutely sure.

'As for Jennifer,' Fran was wry, 'she might double-dare herself to go into the library, but she wasn't angry with Sylvia. Jennifer thinks if she looks appealing enough everyone will be nice to her. Her double-dares are simply for moments of drama. But consider this, Cheerful Voice. What if Sylvia was alive when I went inside. What if I killed her?'

I was irritated. 'Of course you didn't.'

She looked intrigued. 'How do you know for certain?'

'You are innocent or I wouldn't be here. The Department of Good Intentions protects the innocent.'

'The Department of Good Intentions.' The words wobbled a bit. 'I'd like to believe you.'

I reached out, took her hands in mine, held them tight for a moment.

When I loosened my grasp, she managed a smile. 'Thank you. With you on my side, maybe' – again that word wobbled – 'maybe the police won't come back.'

'Perhaps not.' I like to be encouraging. 'All the police have is circumstantial evidence. You were there, but so were a bunch of people with equal opportunity. As long as the police don't find a compelling motive, you are safe.'

'Motive?' Her tone was bleak. 'Oh. God.'

'Excuse me.' The deep voice was puzzled. 'Are you on speakerphone?'

We both jerked toward the door.

Fran stared at Don Smith. She might have looked the same if she stood at the steps to a guillotine. The police. Here. Now. The imprint of past sorrows was evident in the depths of her gray eyes, the vulnerable droop of her lips. She lifted a hand to her throat as he walked across the room, his steps slow and heavy.

He loomed above her. 'I'm off duty.' His words were firm, but his face was that of a man unsure of his welcome.

'Off duty.' She repeated the words as if part of an unknown exotic language.

'Off duty.' Spoken with urgent force.

They gazed at each other, a man and a woman with their own particular stories of love and loss. He was tall, dark-haired, firm featured, a broad forehead, strong nose, blunt chin. Lines etched at the corners of his mouth suggested he'd faced hardship, might harbor painful memories. There was intelligence and empathy in his dark eyes. She looked as though she might once have been quick and eager and full of laughter, but those days were now just a memory.

'I'm off duty.' He repeated the words, his voice deep and strong.

She glanced around the store. 'Can I interest you in a porcelain vase? A gift for your wife?'

He spoke slowly. 'Gretchen died two years ago. Two years. Three months. Eighteen days.'

'I'm sorry.' The warmth in her voice was genuine, acknowledged how much loss hurts. Her eyes held understanding.

'Thank you.'

I'm sorry and *thank you* are often automatic, with no emotional engagement. Not this time. She was sorry deep within. Her response touched him and his gratitude was heartfelt.

The tightness eased from his shoulders. 'I didn't come to shop. I wanted to tell you that Judy Weitz is my friend. And yours. "One who knows how to show and accept kindness will be a friend better than any possession." I don't remember dates and battles and chronology from Bill Loring's classes. I remember the quotes he liked to share. That's one of my favorites.'

Her lips curved in a quick smile. 'Bill was a quote machine. I always botch them when I try to remember. I think what intrigued me the most when Bill talked about Cicero or Socrates is how real they were to me. He understood that people are people and it doesn't matter if they lived in 40 BC or now.'

Don was eager. 'In his class, I felt like Cicero was sitting beside me, giving me a quizzical look, maybe straightening his toga or drinking a glass of wine. Another good man who died violently.'

'Violence.' Fran was somber. 'The same then as now.'

'Yeah.' Don gave a shrug. 'That's the downer to being a cop. Too much bad turns you hard. But the bad makes you value the good. Like Judy. She does her job, had to ID you when she saw the security clip. And she can't hide what she knows about you and Sylvia Chandler. She talked to Gustavus Baldwin. She has to turn in her report but she said she has a lot of other stuff to deal with today so she won't get her report written until late so it likely won't be read until Monday.'

'Gustavus Baldwin.' Fran's tone was bitter.

Don spoke quickly. 'The report will be neutral, maybe say you disagreed with some of Sylvia's actions as a Goddard trustee. No red flag there.'

'Sylvia and Gus stole days from Bill.' The words were heavy with anguish.

'The report will be a recital of facts. No conclusions drawn. As sloppy as the department's being run now, nobody may ever read Judy's report. Right now you're OK. Judy will keep her report to a minimum. Maybe a miracle will occur before Monday morning. But listen up, if you are arrested, don't make a peep without a lawyer. Right now it's Friday morning and you need a break. How about we go to Pawhuska, have lunch at Ree Drummond's Mercantile?'

Fran stared at him uncertainly. 'I know you're off duty. But can police go on outings with suspects?'

His generous mouth broadened in a huge smile. 'Maybe I'll rewrite the manual, underline the necessity to consider character when investigating. You want the truth? As far as Detective Don Smith is concerned, Bill Loring's widow is not a criminal. Not now. Not ever. As far as Detective Don Smith is concerned, suspecting you is stupid. I don't do stupid.'

Fran's lips curved in a quick smile. 'I'll take that as a tribute to Bill. Thank you.' Her gray eyes studied him. 'I have a feeling you may not do stupid, but you have a soft spot for a cat trapped in a tree or an old lady trying to cross a street and this time you're giving me a boost because of Bill. I probably should say no. I shouldn't make your life complicated. But I'd love to go. I'd love to drive away from everything that's happened and be with a nice man and have a great lunch. So yes, I'll go with you.' She pulled out a desk drawer, retrieved her purse, stood. She quickly lifted a jacket from a coat tree, slipped into it. Her thin face was eager. On the way out, she flipped the Open sign, and they were out the door, his hand at her elbow.

I smiled as Don's gorgeous car pulled away from the curb, heading for the highway leaving darkness behind them. The almost three-hour drive to Pawhuska would give them time to talk, to discover each other. I was curious about their destination. An Emporium? But it was many years since I'd been to Pawhuska. Of course there would be changes. In any event, they could be free and happy.

Free and happy until Monday when AC Howie Harris would seize on Judy Weitz's report. All he needed for an arrest was a motive for Fran.

I turned on all the lights in Sam's office, nudged the thermostat to 72. Despite the waft of warm air from the registers and the harsh fluorescent glare from the ceiling, Sam's office seemed cheerless. I longed for the rumble of Sam's deep voice as we sat on the old brown leather sofa. The office was alien without Sam's presence.

Even more concerning, Howie Harris was making a mess of a murder investigation and he was actively conspiring to get Sam's job. Sam needed to know. I thought, *Sam's car.*

The familiar four-door brown sedan was parked in the graveled drive of a modest white frame house on a quiet street with elms and an excited terrier chasing a rabbit. I could have been in any small town in Oklahoma. Frame houses, modest residences, modest lives.

In the living room, Sam's wife Claire was seated in a chintz-covered chair near a small heater, a Bible open in her lap. The furniture was old, worn, clean, tidy. Photographs in plastic frames offered smiling faces, memories of happy times, bits and pieces of particular moments in time. Claire's face held sadness, acceptance.

Sam was in the front bedroom with white dimity curtains at the two windows, a brown oak dresser and vanity, and a bookcase filled with more framed pictures. He sat beside a double bed. He held in one large hand the small hand of the elderly woman lying quite still beneath a red-and-white quilt.

I gazed at the woman's face, a big broad face and likely the hair now loose on the pillow had been coal black like Sam's. He was a masculine replica of the woman.

She stirred, opened dark brown eyes.

He bent forward. 'I'm here, Mom.'

She looked at him for a quiet moment, smiled and slipped again into sleep.

Sam was absent for the best reason in the world. Sam was absent from his post because of love.

I paused long enough in the living room to gaze over Claire's shoulder, read the verse touched by her finger:

Philippians 4:8. Finally, brethren, whatever is true, whatever is honorable, whatever is right, whatever is pure, whatever is lovely, whatever is of good repute, if there is any excellence and if anything worthy of praise, let your mind dwell on these things.

I can't imagine a greater tribute from a daughter-in-law to her husband's mother.

I returned to Sam's office. I carried with me the sober realization that I was on my own. Saving Fran was my mission. I shrugged away Wiggins's cryptic parting words *Don and . . .* and settled behind Sam's desk. As I pulled out the M&M drawer to retrieve the printout of Don's report, I felt reassured. Maybe Wiggins meant Don and I would save Fran. Right this minute Don and Fran were likely curving around a grove of bois d'arc on their way to Pawhuska. I was ready for a moment of cheer.

Fran was smiling. 'It may be my favorite place in all the world. Trees on the cliffs bent by the wind. Fog rolling in from the sea. Cold as an ice chest in August. Bill and I went to Carmel every summer.'

'Gretchen and I spent two weeks in the wine country a few years ago. She loved rosé. That was before the fires.'

The Corvette clung to a curve, traveling fast. Sun speared through Fran's window and the little redwood house hanging from the rear-view mirror gleamed.

Fran reached out, touched the charm. 'This looks like a tiny replica of a house. A very different house.'

Don glanced at the charm, straightened the car from the curve. 'Gretchen was an architect. Her dream house. Our dream house. I'd like to show you the house.' His face was open, unguarded. 'One day soon.'

Fran gently cupped the swaying charm in her fingers. 'One day soon.'

At Sam's desk, I repeated the words like a mantra. *One day soon . . .* I slid out the M&M drawer, picked up the sheets of Don's report and the M&M sack. The crunchy candies seemed to repeat *One day soon . . . One day soon . . .* I arranged the sheets in order, looked first at the dossier on Sylvia Cramer Chandler.

Sylvia Cramer Chandler
B. 3 September 1970, Phoenix, AZ. Graduate Arizona State University. Worked for a realty firm in Scottsdale while in school, full-time upon graduation. Became a million-dollar seller two years out of college. Established her own real-estate firm, Yellow Road Realty, in 1995. Married Wilbur Lane in 1998. No children. Divorced in 2002. Sold Arthur Chandler a condo in 2004. Married Arthur, a widower, six months later. Arthur inherited Chandler Exploration which was founded by his grandfather, Thomas Chandler. Sylvia was fascinated by the oil and gas business, made a point of mastering the intricacies of both exploration and production. She soon was Arthur's chief assistant and became a vice president of the company in 2007. Sylvia loved Adelaide, said four seasons were better than hot and hotter. Sylvia was active in community projects, everything from a food pantry to the Art League to Community Chest. She and Arthur enjoyed golf, sailing, and an occasional trip to

Paris. After her husband's stroke, Sylvia assumed control of Chandler Exploration. She was on the Goddard Board of Trustees. Chandler's three adult children arrived at the home last week after their father suffered another stroke. Arthur is now under the care of a hospice. Arthur's longtime executive secretary Margaret Foster also resides at the house.

'Howie Harris needs to investigate everyone who was in the house last night, not just Fran.' I spoke aloud. Forcefully. I've lived long enough and I've served as an emissary from the department often enough to avoid declarative pronouncements. Except when I know I'm right. Just as Detective Don Smith announced that Bill Loring's widow was not a criminal. Not now. Not ever. I agreed.

I remembered Fran's dismissive laugh when I said Travis and Jennifer were family and surely they would step up if she was arrested and admit their presence at the Chandler house before Fran arrived.

Surely one of them would. Unless Travis was a murderer and his wife was protecting him.

SIX

Travis Roberts knocked on the bedroom door.

'Jennifer.' His voice was loud, almost harsh, but there was an underlying plea.

Silence.

He rubbed large knuckles across a jutting jawbone. His face was twisted in uncertainty, tinged with anger. He was haggard, looked as if he'd tossed and turned the whole night through. Perhaps that was why he was still at home. His unshaven cheeks bristled with dark stubble, his long hair was tangled, poking out at odd angles. He was barefoot in a ragged T-shirt and red-and black striped boxer shorts.

'Open the door.' He rattled the knob.

Silence.

'Dammit, talk to me.'

Silence.

'All I did was take her a painting. I can't help it that somebody killed her. Listen, it doesn't have anything to do with us.'

Silence.

'I got home as soon as I could. The police took forever.'

Silence.

'Jennifer?'

Silence.

Inside the bedroom the light was dim. Jennifer huddled in a velvet-covered chair, her cotton candy-cane patterned nightgown bunched over her knees. Her brown hair straggled on her shoulders. Her face was starkly bare of makeup. She stared at the floor and held a bunny house shoe over each ear.

The door shook in its frame as he pounded.

She hunkered deeper in the chair, pressed the house shoes tighter against her ears.

'Jenn, talk to me.'

Silence.

* * *

I stood in front of the blackboard in Sam's office. I picked up the chalk, printed in bold letters.

Intruders on the Chandler terrace in order of arrival.
Travis Roberts
Jennifer Roberts
Fran Loring

It was as if Sam stood at my elbow. I printed:

Residents of Chandler House
Elise Chandler Douglas
Dwight Douglas
Crystal Chandler Pace
Jason Pace
Stuart Chandler
Margaret Foster
Arthur Chandler and attendant

Sam would interview each one. He would dig and delve, figure out who wanted Sylvia to die and why. Why Sylvia? Why now?

At the desk, I grabbed the M&Ms, poured a handful, crunched, and spread out the sheets from Don's report on Sam's desk.

Nine-one-one call received at eight forty-seven p.m. Sylvia Chandler last seen alive at approximately seven fifty p.m. by attendant to her husband, Arthur. Residing in the house at the time of her death were Arthur Chandler, who is bedridden and comatose, and his attendant, Arthur's two daughters and their spouses, his son, and a longtime executive secretary.

Elise Chandler Douglas, 48. Husband Dwight Douglas, 50. Dallas, TX. They'd stand out in a lineup. Hers is a face only a plastic surgeon and a vain woman could love. She has that treat-me-special-I'm-rich vibe, the kind of woman who looks down a long nose and snaps, 'That's unacceptable.' She owns a high-end dress shop. He runs a lumber company. Hunts elk and bears in Wyoming. Lots of FB photos, him and carcasses. Big dude. Hard face. He comes across as shove-a-shiv-in-your-back mean. Both said nice things about Sylvia Chandler, but they are not the kind of people you want to cross.

I was surprised and then I wasn't. Detective Don Smith wasn't sending Sam background as in schooling, residence, credit rating. He was sending Sam his judgment based on years of contact with good people and bad.

Crystal Chandler Pace, 46. Husband Jason Pace, 49. St Louis, MO. She's involved, a fluff of her hands, in oh-so-many community activities, women's health, the arts, her sorority, president of the Women's Tennis League at the club. And, of course, the children, Junior and Cissy and Tessie. So much to see to but she stays fit. Tennis. Missouri Valley doubles two years ago. He was about the same, men's group at the club, golf, tennis. Sure missing the men's grill. The fellas been texting when am I coming back. The Paces take precious good care of themselves. She's thin, he's tanned. Know all the latest shows, wouldn't recognize a job if they fell over it. Takes a heft of money to support that lifestyle.

Don's disdain was clear. He saw them as potted plants requiring rich soil. He didn't picture either raising a poker to strike Sylvia. But clearly both were athletic and fit and quite capable of wielding tennis racquets and golf clubs. Those same muscles would bring a poker down with strength and precision.

Stuart Barton Chandler, 37. No current abode. Separated from his wife, Melissa, who's living in their house in Ardmore. Son, Jimmy, 16. Daughter, Phoebe, 12. Chandler's been staying at the Chandler home on Lake Texoma. My little sister dragged around a cloth Eeyore until she was almost twelve. Scruffy, lopsided, tail missing. But the damn thing charmed everybody she met. That's Stu Chandler. Needs a haircut. Pudgy. Would always take the elevator, not the stairs. Probably has a couple of bottles stashed in his room. You can smell whisky. But he has a quick grin even when his head is pounding. Only problem, sometimes it's a good old boy who lashes out. Then chugs another drink.

Was Stu Chandler's had-too-much-to-drink a ploy to mask a clever killer? He seemed genuine, unaffected, possibly a little bumptious. There was fondness in his tone when he mentioned Sylvia Chandler. Was that also duplicitous? And as he climbed the stairs last night, I remembered his mutter, 'In the nick of time, but that's a crime.' The words thick and almost inaudible. But I heard them.

Margaret Foster – If an iceberg was bearing down on a ship, she'd be a great skipper. Cool. Collected. No trappings of wealth or power. The kind of woman you'd trust with the family silver. She appeared shocked by the crime, kept saying, 'Dreadful. So dreadful.' She said Sylvia's death will be a blow to the company. Foster's been the executive secretary for almost twenty-five years. As for living at the house, she said Arthur and his wife, Ellen, took her in after her husband's death. She'd planned to be a temporary guest but they were congenial and she'd stayed on and never regretted it. Foster said Sylvia was a workaholic and loved running the company and ran it very well. 'More money every year.' Said with approval. 'And generous. She just recently made a substantial gift to Goddard College. Of course, she was a trustee.'

Goddard College kindly provided visitors with a campus map. The history department was housed in the Arts and Sciences building. I checked the ground floor directory. Gustavus Baldwin, chair of the history department, was in Room 203. I was alone in the hall outside his door. I chose a black suit, ivory blouse, and low black leather heels. For luck, I added a gold link chain with a gold four-leaf clover.

I knocked.

'Not office hours yet.' A grumpy male voice.

I glanced at the placard next to the door. Office Hours 2–4 p.m.

Sweet work if you can get it.

I grabbed the knob, turned, entered.

Instant antipathy. I didn't like his full head of stiff black hair, his fish-slab face or his bushy beard.

Pale green eyes reminiscent of pond algae speared me. 'Whatever it is, I don't want any.'

I pulled a soft leather ID folder from one pocket, flashed it. 'Detective M. Loy.' In the past I aided Sam as Patrol Officer M. Loy, the name a tribute to the redheaded actress who starred with William Powell in the irrepressible Nick and Nora Charles movies inspired by Dashiell Hammett's *The Thin Man*.

Baldwin clawed at his beard, snapped, 'I told the gal this morning, none of it was a big deal. Except Bill's widow decided to raise a fuss, like relieving a sick man from teaching was a crime. Loring was a dead man walking. Creepy. But he kept meeting his classes. Sylvia thought a terminally ill prof was a big downer for kids. She came to me since I was acting head of the department. I agreed with Sylvia. I told Bill I'd take his classes. And I did. Fran acted like I was some kind of a usurper. Sylvia said I handled everything masterfully.'

I walked closer to his desk. 'You knew Mrs Chandler well?'

'I'd met her around. I haven't seen her in a month or so.' He picked up a pen, rolled it between his fingers. 'Sylvia was very interested in the school. She took being a trustee seriously.'

And you, I thought coolly, would go out of your way to please a powerful trustee.

'Fran Loring came to see me after Bill died.' A resentful glare. 'She accused me of stealing days from his life, said the classes gave him reason to hold on, he would have lived longer. Absolute rot.' His eyes glittered with dislike. 'Like I told the detective, if you're looking for somebody unbalanced who resented Sylvia Chandler, check out Fran Loring.'

'We are checking out a good many people. Where were you last night at eight o'clock?' Sylvia was last seen alive at ten to eight. Margaret Foster and Travis Roberts called nine-one-one at eight forty-seven.

'Teaching a night class.'

I took the particulars and turned away.

Judy Weitz might couch her report in neutral language, but Howie Harris would see enough to visit Gustavus Baldwin. I remembered Howie Harris's eagerness at breakfast. All he needed was a motive.

Fran was certain to be arrested unless Jennifer and Travis Roberts stated that Sylvia Chandler was dead before Fran stepped on to the terrace at twenty-two minutes after eight.

Jennifer's hand shook as she applied mascara, leaving a streak on one cheek. Her fluffy brown hair was brushed and framed her rounded face. She stared in the mirror. 'I won't look like this. I won't. I won't.' She picked up another brush and added color to her cheeks. In a moment or two, she looked better. She touched the shiny bangle necklace at her throat, bright against a dark blue sweater. Abruptly, she pushed up from the bench in front of the vanity, hurried across the bedroom. The bed was unmade.

I glanced at the covers. Rather clearly she'd not shared the bed last night, the covers rumpled on only one side. She flung open the closet door, darted inside, returned with a wheeled suitcase. She threw the case on the foot of the bed, opened it.

On the front porch I Appeared in the modest black suit. I put my finger on the doorbell, pressed and held.

She opened the front door, said, 'I don't want any.'

Before she could shut the door, I planted my foot firmly on the sill as I flashed the ID. 'Detective M. Loy. A few questions about last night, Mrs Roberts.'

'Last night?' Her voice was faint.

'You were on the Chandler terrace.'

Those blue eyes weren't vacant now. They were wide and desperate and determined. 'I have no idea what you're talking about.' She didn't budge, blocking my entrance to the front hall.

'A security camera filmed you at the door to the library.' Of course she had no way of knowing the cameras didn't cover either the library door or the stairway to the terrace.

She shook her head, the soft brown hair rippling. 'There's some mistake. You have the wrong address. I was home last night. In my room.' Her voice grew stronger. 'The most dreadful headache ever. Sorry I can't help you.'

'You were there.'

She turned away, flung over her shoulder. 'You've made a mistake. I was here all evening.'

As she had last night, she picked up speed, her shoes slapping against the floor. She reached the hall and in a moment a door slammed.

I slipped the leather ID folder into my pocket. In a way I had to hand it to her. She would never admit to her journey up the hill last night, no matter what evidence contradicted her.

Likely Jennifer had made her way through life, school, dates, family tensions, by blindly, stubbornly negating culpability. Was this just another instance of escapism or was she grimly sloughing off murder in the only way she knew how?

The Closed sign faced outward at the Roberts Art Gallery. Carefully placed lighting illuminated paintings on three walls. Another time I would have enjoyed looking at the paintings, colors vivid as macaw feathers or rubies sparkling in sunlight, a kayaker cresting crystal water, a hammock between two palm trees, boarded-up shops on a desolate street, a wolf, yellowish teeth bared, poised to spring. I moved near the far wall and Appeared.

I made no effort to be quiet, instead purposefully stepped firmly on the parquet floor toward a doorway with a beaded curtain. I pushed the rippling beads aside.

Travis Roberts jerked around from an easel, glared. He held a brush in his right hand. 'The Gallery's closed. Get out.' In a spear of sunshine from a skylight his prominent nose and jawbones reminded me of the painting of the wolf, predatory, dangerous.

I flashed the ID folder. 'Detective M. Loy.' My tone was

crisp, businesslike. 'Tell me again about your talk last night with Sylvia Chandler. Why did you call her?'

'She was the director of the Summer Art Festival and I wanted to show her a painting that's perfect for the poster.'

'What time did you talk to her?'

He swung to pick up a cell phone from a side table, glanced, tapped. 'At eight oh-three.'

'Did she sound as usual?'

He blinked. 'Oh yeah. Quick. Decisive.' Sylvia was alive at shortly after eight o'clock.

I stepped nearer, looked hard into his wild dark eyes. 'You didn't tell us about your first visit to the Chandler house last night.'

He hunched his big shoulders, but his face maintained the angry stare. 'You got that wrong. I brought a painting. I wish to hell I'd never gone there.'

'You brought the painting on your second visit to the house.' I made a quick estimate of how long it took Travis to park the car, walk on the path to the stairs, reach the terrace. 'A security camera filmed you on the terrace at thirteen minutes after eight.'

He gestured with the brush. 'You're wasting my time.' He was aggrieved, determined, impatient. 'I can't help you. It doesn't matter if I was on the terrace earlier. I started to go in, changed my mind, decided to get the painting. I came here, got it, went to the house. I don't know anything about what happened to Sylvia. You better see who gets richer because she's dead. Not me.' The two words were flung at me. 'She was doing great things for my work. And now you can get out.' He turned his back on me.

His head bent forward, the brush made a streak of coral on the canvas. He was in another world. For him, I didn't exist, the room didn't exist, nothing in life existed for him at this moment but that canvas and the brush in his hand.

'You were furious with Sylvia.' My tone was accusatory. 'You stormed into the library. Did you kill her?'

He appeared oblivious to the sound of my voice. A police inquiry didn't matter to him. I rather thought the fact of murder didn't matter. He was painting. He didn't care. He would never care. I felt a chill. He would always do whatever he thought he must do to paint. Last night if he confronted Sylvia, would her ability to help him in the future outweigh his fury at losing top billing at the festival?

'You have exactly five minutes to tell me every step you took.'

He swung to face me. His brooding glare and hunched shoulders told me he was wild for me to leave, that he had a vision, he wanted me gone. 'OK, OK. I'll tell you what happened then you can get the hell out of here. I stepped inside, yelled her name. No answer. I decided to go get my new painting, show her, make her see this painting would be the best at the festival. I went back out on the terrace. It was real quiet.' His voice held a memory of silence. 'I heard the click of a door. I thought oh hell, what if somebody's coming out? I could see the kitchen door in the lights. It's bright yellow. It was closed. But it was darker than hell on the other side of the terrace, the west wing. I wondered if somebody was standing there. I didn't want to waste time talking to anybody so I got the hell off the terrace. I wanted to get to the gallery, get my painting, get back, show her. I ducked down and ran for the steps. I went down fast and ran on to my car. I drove here. I got the painting and went back. I didn't bother to say I'd been there earlier because it didn't matter.'

'You called Sylvia a little after eight.'

'Yeah, yeah.'

'She was alive.'

His look was contemptuous. 'So far as I know dead people don't talk. Yeah. She was alive.' He breathed impatience.

'You arrive maybe ten minutes later and call out and she doesn't respond.'

'Yeah.' His dark eyes were defiant. He wasn't going to admit he stormed inside and found her dead. Or stormed inside and left her dead.

I attacked, my voice hard. 'You either killed her or you found her dead.'

The muscles tightened in his big blunt face. Those dark

eyes burned. 'I gave a yell. She didn't answer. Yeah, I guess she could have been dead.'

The knowledge hung between us. He knew she was dead when he stepped outside.

'You heard a door shut. And you ran.'

'Yeah.'

'Did you see anyone?' Only a monumental ego focused on his own actions would fail to understand that the sound of a closing door only the length of a house from a dead woman might be very important.

'Like I said, I didn't have time to fool with anyone. So I ran. Anyway, that's all I know.' He turned to the canvas.

'Why did you run?' A cold skeptical voice.

A whiff of coal smoke tickled my nose.

'In a hurry. To get the painting.'

Yes, he was in a hurry. Travis ran for the steps. If he killed Sylvia Chandler, he was desperate not to be seen in the light spilling out from the library windows. If he found her dead, he didn't want to raise the alarm because he knew only too well that she must have been killed within moments of his arrival.

A door closed.

Did Sylvia's murderer hear Travis coming up the steps, watch him enter the library and hurriedly depart? If so, the murderer was not an outsider. The murderer lived in the Chandler house.

Coal smoke intensified. 'Don't leave town, Mr Roberts.' A stern warning.

I brushed through the beaded doorway. Coal smoke engulfed me. As the curtain rippled behind me, I announced, 'Sam's office,' and disappeared.

I was a little breathless as I sank on to Sam's old brown leather sofa. I composed my face as I Appeared and attempted to look demure.

The other end of the sofa squeaked as Wiggins sat down.

'Bailey Ruth.' His voice was heavy with disappointment. 'Precept Six.'

'Talking to a voice unnerves me.' Especially a voice
weighted with disapproval.

A long pause. Finally colors swirled.

I always took comfort from his stalwart appearance, the
blue cap with a black bill perched atop thick reddish hair, his
florid face with spaniel brown eyes and luxuriant sideburns
and handlebar mustache. Today, his face was puckered with
dismay and he sat stiffly with broad hands firmly planted on
the knees of his gray flannel trousers.

'Precept Six.' A voice of doom. 'Make every effort not to
alarm earthly creatures.'

'Wiggins, I—'

'A flagrant, egregious violation.' Wiggins was always courteous. That he interrupted me signaled enormous displeasure.
'Bailey Ruth.' The syllables dropped with the finality of dirt
clods on a coffin lid, presaging a brusque pronouncement of
dismissal as an emissary. 'That frightened girl.' Wiggins is
chivalrous. And Jennifer's ostrich act likely evoked sympathy
from him. 'And that artist struggling to answer his muse. I
never thought I would see an emissary deliberately distress
earthly creatures. That poor young woman unable to cope with
such an attack. That poor young man driven to share his vision
with the world through his brush and canvas.'

I flung decorum out the window, responded hotly. 'That
poor young woman and that poor young man have it in their
power to protect an innocent woman but neither one will tell
the truth. Wiggins, I can't be sweetness and light this time.
I'm the only hope Fran Loring has.'

'My dear Bailey Ruth,' Wiggins sounded forbearing, 'Fran
is innocent.'

Coal smoke swirled.

'You know she's innocent. I know she's innocent. We don't
matter. The acting chief is convinced the murderer came from
the terrace. He has a color photo from the security camera
that shows Fran on the terrace at eight twenty-two. That young
man left his house after speaking to Sylvia on the phone. He
arrived on the terrace a few minutes later. He wasn't filmed
by the security camera because he came up the main steps to
the terrace. His wife Jennifer heard him running as he left.

She too came up to the terrace, tied the dog to the railing of the steps. I think she also entered the library and saw the body. If she or Travis tell what they know, Fran will be cleared of any suspicion. That's why I spoke sternly to them. Monday morning Howie Harris will pounce on a motive for Fran and she'll be arrested. Wiggins,' I was adamant, 'Detective M. Loy is the only one on the case. I have to scrap and fight for information if I'm to save Fran. I know I scared Jennifer. I doubt I rattled Travis. The man paints, in case you haven't noticed, and painting is all that matters to him: not murder, not his sister, nothing else. Maybe,' my voice wobbled, 'I'll have to be tough with more people before I'm through. I can't always be the good cop. You know how that works. One cop is kind and encouraging. The other cop acts like a brute. I don't have any help. I'm on my own. If I have to scrap to save Fran, I will.'

His face softened. He reached out, patted my shoulder. 'How difficult for you.' There was sympathy in his voice.

Wiggins should have seen me handle the football player in the last row of my class. I learned tough a long time ago.

His spaniel brown eyes were kind. 'Dear Bailey Ruth. Circumstances alter cases. Do what you must to save Fran.'

Coal smoke thickened. His voice was fading. 'But that's not the most important task. Don and . . .'

Wiggins was gone.

Don and . . .

'Wiggins? *Don and . . .*'

There was no answer.

I looked about in amazement. I remembered Pawhuska as a charming little town with only an occasional pedestrian and a few shops, a feed store the largest, and an occasional pick-up on the street. Now cars were bumper to bumper and the sidewalks were crowded.

I tagged along behind a group of fortyish women oohing and aahing. 'Do you suppose she'll be here today?' 'I hear she has a gorgeous studio out on the ranch to film her TV shows.' 'I never miss her blogs.' 'I saw her once at a signing at The Full Circle bookstore in Oklahoma City.'

We inched forward and I read the legend on the plate glass:

The Pioneer Woman Mercantile

Once through the doors I felt pulled back in time as I surveyed an old-fashioned dry goods store with all kinds of items for sale. Christmas decorations glittered and lights glistened on a tall Christmas tree. Shoppers clutched bags filled to the brim, many with packages gaily wrapped for the holidays. The café was to my left. I spotted Fran and Don in the fourth booth.

I smelled coffee and cinnamon and roasting meats. I stood beside their booth.

Fran lifted her spoon. 'This is as good as my mom's cherry pie and she makes cherry pie fit for angels.'

I suppressed a sigh. I love cherry pie.

Don scraped the dessert plate for a last morsel. 'Couldn't be any better than the coconut cream pie.' He lifted his coffee cup. 'Do you like to cook, Fran?'

She put the spoon on the plate. 'I used to. I haven't cooked in a while. Was Gretchen a good cook?'

Don grinned. 'Gretchen was a math whiz. The kitchen, not so much. Actually I did most of the cooking. I like to grill. How about Bill?'

Fran held up both hands in mock horror. 'He meant well. I didn't even trust him to boil water. He forgot my tea kettle and when I smelled it burning and came running, he said, "The most amazing thing about the Carthaginians . . ."' She laughed.

Don leaned forward. 'Maybe I could have you over for a T-bone sometime.'

She looked at his eager face and said softly, 'I'd like that, Don. Very much.'

As Mama always told us kids, 'Happiness is often in moments that seem small in the scheme of larger life, but small moments make up a life.' Fran and Don were living a small happy moment. I wasn't needed here. And that made me happy, too.

I can only resist so much temptation. I was starving and the café was so appealing. The aromas of good food superbly cooked proved irresistible. I ducked behind a pillar and Appeared. I enjoyed every mouthful of delectable ravioli. And, of course, cherry pie.

SEVEN

Afternoon sunlight streamed through a skylight and the silver nymph in the entrance hall fountain gleamed. Water arched from a spout in the nymph's graceful hands. The soft splash was cheerful, soothing. 'Blue Danube' played on a sound system. There was no hint here that a woman died violently the night before.

I made a quick check of the entire house. I walked through the living area where the family gathered last night. Between two dusty tapestries I found closed double doors. I opened them to a hallway. The first room contained a pool table, a ping-pong table, and two pinball machines. The next room was an office. A fire crackled in a small fireplace. Crisp white curtains framed three windows with a view of late-blooming pansies. Margaret Foster sat at the golden oak desk. She straightened her glasses as she rapidly flipped pages of a document. She appeared as she had the evening before, composed, serious, intelligent. Perhaps she found a moment of relief immersed in work.

In the next room, a deer head was mounted on one wall next to a dartboard. The room was a clubby-looking retreat with leather sofas and a fireplace. The surroundings spoke of cheer over drinks. There was a faint scent of cigar smoke. Stuart Chandler slumped on a leather sofa. On an end table to his right was a half-filled glass next to a fifth of bourbon. He held a cell phone. He stared at the phone, his face forlorn.

Next door was an exercise room with machines, pulleys, weights, a simulated rower, that appeared austere in contrast. The last door opened to an indoor swimming pool. Deckchairs clustered near the deep end. Pool toys of every sort were visible in a netted enclosure. I leaned over, swept my hand through the water. Salt water. I looked up at a high dive with a long board.

I returned to the expansive marbled entrance hall. Beyond

the fountain an archway opened to a magnificent dining room. The polished oak table could easily seat twenty. Two sideboards and three china cabinets affirmed the ability to entertain. A swinging door led into a large kitchen.

A gray-haired woman with a red-and-white-checked apron over a white blouse and turquoise slacks expertly wielded a potato peeler. She spoke excitedly into a cell phone tucked between chin and shoulder. '. . . could have knocked me over with a feather. If you haven't watched Channel 5, turn it on. They've got pictures of her. Not the way they found her, but pictures of her and Mr Chandler at their place at Lake Tahoe. You know how they loved to sail. Just so awful. She was all business but she was fair and she always complimented me on a special dish. She said my biscuits were the best in the world. I heard she was all bunched up on the sofa . . . Last night I left early because it's Bunny's birthday. Mrs Chandler was swell about when I needed time for something special. They say she was killed sometime after eight. She sang to Mr Chandler every night. The attendant said she started downstairs about ten to eight. Mrs Foster and that artist found her body in the library around eight forty-five . . . Scary to think I was that close to being here. I usually finish up around eight thirty. But not last night . . .' The kitchen-sink window overlooked the terrace. The door that opened to the terrace was shut. I suspected it was firmly locked.

I returned to the main entrance hall and crossed to double doors exactly like those that opened to the long hall in the west wing. These doors led to the hallway to the east wing. The first room was a huge office with two distinctive desks. An old knotty pine likely belonged to Arthur's grandfather who established Chandler Exploration. The other desk was painted bright yellow. A poster on a wall proclaimed Yellow Brick Road Realty. Sylvia brought her yellow road with her to Adelaide. Structure contour maps showing geologic formations hung on three walls. The fourth was filled with framed photographs of Arthur and later Arthur and Sylvia in hard hats visiting drilling sites.

The surface of the knotty pine desk was bare. On the yellow desk, the in- and out-box on one corner held papers. Several folders were ranged on one side. A pen rested atop a legal pad and several folders. I moved nearer, looked down at the legal pad:

Lunch at faculty club next Thursday.

Get some honeysuckle for Arthur.

When sale goes through, bonus packages for all employees.

Call Chuck re. sale.

Endow Chair at OU in honor of Arthur?

I opened the first folder. Printouts of e-mail exchanges revealed Sylvia was deep in negotiations with Devon to sell Chandler Exploration. A cover letter from local attorney Charles Vinson summarized a proposed acquisition agreement.

'A damn shame. She was a fine woman. I thought the world of her.'

Charles Vinson's office was lawyerly, with case books and treatises shelved in dark wooden bookcases. As a gentleman would, he remained standing until I settled in a chair facing his desk. Tall and thin, he looked like an elderly stork in a beautifully tailored gray suit. He lowered himself stiffly, likely an aging back, into a cushiony black leather chair. He sighed. 'I can't think what Adelaide's coming to. A woman in her own home not bothering anybody. I talked to the police this morning. No reports of any vagrants. I understand some woman was caught on security footage. It's hard to believe a woman would do something like that.'

'I understand Sylvia was negotiating with Devon to sell Chandler Exploration.'

His rather dour features spread in a smile. 'First-rate negotiator. Started at eighteen million. I thought she'd be lucky to get twelve. Those people know their business. But she held tight at sixteen and by God they agreed. A good company for them. One hundred and eighteen working wells producing oil from the Dykeman formation and interests in 209 wells. Of course the leases include the Woodford shale and that's a big draw for deep drillers like Devon.'

'How does this affect the Chandler family?'

'A huge payout.' A touch of awe in his voice.

'Was any member of the family opposed to the sale?'

Vinson gave a dry chuckle. 'You mean hang on to the company for sentimental reasons? The Chandlers take money over sentiment any day of the week. I spoke to Elise this morning. She's the oldest and of course she's concerned about her dad and trying to decide about Sylvia's memorial. She didn't mention the sale. The next meeting with Devon is in early December.'

'What happens to Sylvia's estate?'

'Everything to Arthur.'

'If he had predeceased her, what would have happened to his estate?'

Vinson was judicious. 'I rather cautioned Arthur about his decision. But Arthur believed in self-reliance. It was a matter of pride to him that all of his children succeed on their own. When he inherited Chandler Exploration, the company was teetering on bankruptcy. There were some lean years but he, and later he and Sylvia, built it into a major independent oil company. When he started having the strokes, he decided to give Sylvia a life interest in the estate. He said, "The kids are doing fine. No hurry for them to inherit and Sylvia will increase the estate value. I know she will." He said all the children were doing well, Elise with her shop. Dwight's lumber company, Crystal a stay-at-home mother but Jason with his own silver spoon. Stuart's in advertising.'

A life interest to a woman of middle age in excellent health. So long as Sylvia lived, any inheritance for Arthur's children was in a distant future.

But now . . .

'Were the children aware that Sylvia would have a life interest in the estate?'

He looked uncomfortable. 'Elise came to see me on Tuesday. Of course, Arthur's death is imminent and she wanted to find out about the estate. I assumed the family was aware of Arthur's decision.' He shook his head. 'I have to say she was incredulous when she learned that none of the heirs would access any funds as long as Sylva lived.' He stopped. Perhaps hearing his own dry voice and the import of his words shocked him . . . *as long as Sylvia lived.*

Sylvia no longer lived.

Abruptly he continued. 'She asked how I could let this happen. I told her Arthur was adamant and I do what my clients demand. After all, Sylvia was hugely helpful to the growth in recent years. Arthur had great faith in her abilities. Maybe he didn't think any of the children would do as well for the company. In any event, Sylvia had a life interest.'

'And now that Sylvia is dead?'

'Oh,' he was brisk, 'the life interest ended with her death. Now the estate will be shared equally among the children.'

'What is the value of Arthur's estate?'

'Approximately twenty-two million.'

If Sylvia had outlived Arthur, Elise, Crystal, and Stuart would have inherited zip, zero, zilch. Now each would reap a little over seven million apiece.

What price murder? Seven million?

A slurred voice echoed in my mind, 'In the nick of time.'

I took another look at Arthur and Sylvia's huge office. In the top right drawer of the yellow desk I found a daybook. I recognized Sylvia's bold printing. I went back a week, looked at the entries. Sylvia commented on a day. These were personal jottings, not financial.

> Sunday – Church without Arthur is always lonely. None of them came with me. He would be disappointed. The doctor said Arthur only has a few more days. His hand is so frail when I hold it.
>
> Monday – Margaret is checking the files for materials we will need to provide to Devon. Of course everything online now. I will miss the company. Perhaps I will write a history of Chandler Exploration. Arthur's grandfather lost one eye in a rig accident, wore a patch, and looked like a pirate. Arthur says those were wild days in the oil patch.
>
> Tuesday – Odd at dinner tonight. A sense of underlying stress. Talk disjointed. Something's going on with the family. But perhaps it's the fact that Arthur has only days to live.

Wednesday – I put the spray of honeysuckle on the pillow.
   I'm sure Arthur smiled.
Thursday – Looked at pictures from Lake Tahoe. I can
   feel the wind in my face and see Arthur at the tiller.
Friday –

I returned the daybook to the drawer.

Before Arthur's stroke he would have spent time in the office, perhaps calling over to Sylvia as she worked at her desk. I imagined him with a booming voice, a voice that could be heard over the clang and roar of a well site. Two vigorous people. Now he was dying and she was dead.

The next room surprised me, a spare room with no drapes, shuttered windows, walls the color of sand, dim lighting, two comfortable easy chairs, and a small table with a handful of large seashells. I picked up a shell, held it to my ear. Of course I heard the roar of the sea. A retreat for contemplation?

Next came a sewing room. A hand-sewn quilt hung on one wall. Knitting needles rested atop a basket of yarn. Sylvia Chandler apparently balanced vigorous activity with periods of quiet, knitting while perhaps listening to music or books.

The last room was the library. Crime tape still sealed the door but was no barrier for me. Sunlight slanted through the tall windows. Last night when Margaret brought Travis to the library, she turned the knob and the door didn't open. I unlocked the door. The locked door made it clear that the murderer left by way of the terrace and that's why Travis heard a door close on the other side of the house when he hurried outside.

The murder occurred between the time Travis called Sylvia and his arrival on the terrace. A short span of time. Either Travis killed her or he found her dead. Did he invent the sound of a closing door to explain why he ran? Or did he hear a door close, signaling the return of the murderer into the Chandler house? I dismissed the possibility Jennifer was the killer because Travis ran. He ran because he was a murderer or he ran because he found Sylvia's body.

If he was innocent, Travis entered the library only a minute or two after the murderer departed.

I stood outside the library on the terrace just as Travis stood last night in a bright splash of light. He claimed he heard a door shut. I glanced at the yellow door into the kitchen, shook my head. That door was clearly visible to him. I turned to gaze at the west wing and the red door at the end. That wing and that door were in dark shadow last night. If Travis heard a click, he heard the red door close. I walked across the terrace to the red door. I used my thumb and index finger to lightly grip either side of the knob. Since I wasn't here, I would not smudge fingerprints, but I was taking no chances. The door was locked. I stepped inside, unlocked the door, returned to the terrace. I used the same maneuver to turn the knob, open the door. I closed the door.

Click.

The crime laboratory at the police station was unoccupied. I breathed a little sigh at the array of equipment, computers, of course, an X-ray, three microscopes, test tubes, iPads. I looked about but found no hint of how orders were processed here.

I thought *Howie's office*. A makeshift sign graced the door: AC Howie Harris. Happily, the office was empty. I supposed his usual spot was in a main area with desks for detectives. His monitor was on. I checked through recent e-mails, noted that Officer Louise Bledsoe was en route to the Chandler house to show the residents the security footage. I checked sent files, found a directive to the laboratory in regard to Fran's boots, I followed the same format and zinged an order down to the Crime Lab: Chandler Homicide – Fingerprint both outer and inner knobs of the red door on the west side of the terrace at the Chandler house. CC results to Chief Cobb. I sent the message then deleted it from the Sent file.

I checked out other e-mails. Howie was keeping the mayor up to date. The most recent message:

Dear Mayor,
Sylvia Chandler's estate reverts to her husband, Arthur.
Elise Chandler Douglas informed me that her father

isn't expected to live more than a few days. The family therefore will remain in Adelaide. Mrs Douglas said a memorial service for Sylvia Chandler is tentatively scheduled for next Thursday.

I am confident we can charge Frances Loring with murder by Tuesday at the latest. I've spoken to the DA and his office agrees. We have an excellent case. He said he can't wait to show the security footage to a jury.

Respectfully yours,
Howie Harris
Acting Chief

I made an instant decision. I opened the right-hand drawer, found a plain sheet of paper. I printed in block letters:

MURDERER RE-ENTERED CHANDLER HOUSE THROUGH WEST WING RED DOOR. THERE IS A WITNESS.

I placed the sheet in the center of his desk. No one can accuse me of hampering a proper police investigation by withholding information.

I shut the center drawer, pulled out the right top drawer. I blinked in surprise when I picked up a book on rhyming. I looked in the bottom drawer and felt a pang. A partially open bag of M&Ms nestled on the bottom, secured by a large red rubber band. I wasn't sure what the candy stash meant. A fellow devotee of M&Ms? An effort to emulate Chief Cobb? I closed the drawer gently.

I pulled out the left top drawer. A stack of loose sheets from a legal pad lay within. It took a moment to decipher rather ornate penmanship and realize I was reading verse. Not very good verse, but verse.

The top sheet:

BLUE
Steadfast we be, all who wear the blue.
Guardians strong, fighting the wrong.
Lift your heads high, always stand tall.
Steadfast be we who wear the blue.

It was like watching a kaleidoscope. The pattern shifted. As Mama always told us kids, 'A plain package don't mean it's empty.'

As I left, I gave the makeshift sign on Howie's door a pat.

A patrol car was parked in the circular drive. The murmur of voices drew me to the living room. Officer Bledsoe, a perky blonde with a cheery smile, placed her laptop on a card table, nodded approval of a huge wall TV.

Most of the residents sat on card-table chairs on either side of the table with a good view of the TV screen. Elise Douglas held a cell phone, tapped a text. Dwight Douglas, long arms dangling, legs outstretched, made the chair seem small. Stuart Chandler stared blankly at a wall. His wispy hair needed a comb and his rounded shoulders slumped. Crystal Pace's bright blonde hair was perky in a ponytail and she looked youthful in rose warmups. She said quietly, 'We appreciate the efficiency of the police. Daddy would be comforted. Except,' her face fell, 'I really don't think he knows any of us now.' Jason Pace in a T-shirt and gym shorts stood behind her chair, rocking on the balls of his feet. 'Need to get my muscles loose.' Margaret Foster stood near the officer. 'Shall I dim the lights?' Margaret's face was pale but she was carefully dressed in a becoming navy wool suit with a pale rose silk blouse.

'The light is fine.' Officer Bledsoe cleared her throat, enjoying her chance to pursue a lead in a murder investigation. 'Ladies and gentlemen, we appreciate your cooperation. The footage I am about to show was taken at twenty-two minutes after eight o'clock last night by the security camera aimed down the east side of the back terrace. Here we go.' She bent to her laptop, tapped.

The image on the screen was fuzzy. She zoomed in and the scene was starkly clear, the time in figures running across the top: 8:20. Light illuminated a portion of flagstones. 8:21. 8:22.

'Oh, look.' Crystal leaned forward.

Fran Loring was on the terrace. She took one step forward, another. She stopped, stared. I thought her face reflected uneasiness, concern. A jury might see her as furtive, threatening.

Abruptly she moved forward, was no longer visible on the screen. 8:23. The terrace was streaked with light and nothing more.

Officer Bledsoe tapped and the screen was blank. 'We are hoping someone here might know—'

Elise interrupted. 'That looks like a woman who has a shop downtown. Lovely silver.' She turned to her sister. 'Do you remember, Crystal? The antique store near Prince Jewelry.'

Margaret said slowly. 'Fran Loring. She owns Mitchell Antiques. Why would she be on the terrace last night?'

Jason did an ankle roll. 'Murderess-in-chief?'

'Mitchell Antiques.' Elise gave a decided nod.

Officer Bledsoe leaned forward. 'Tell me about her.'

Crystal looked puzzled. 'Why do you suppose she was coming to see Sylvia?'

Officer Bledsoe was quick. 'They knew each other?'

'I guess so,' Crystal said uncertainly. She looked at Elise.

Elise was suddenly bored. 'I don't know a thing about her or Sylvia. Sylvia wore very little jewelry.'

'Antiques,' Dwight murmured. 'Not jewelry.'

'Whatever.' Elise gave a dismissive wave.

Jason frowned. 'She didn't look like a woman dropping in for a chat. She looked grim.' Clearly he was referring to Fran.

The officer asked quickly, 'Had Mrs Chandler and Mrs Loring been in contact with each other?'

Jason flexed the fingers on both hands. 'Honey, none of us know squat about who Sylvia saw or didn't. We're all visitors here.'

Elise stood. 'And it's time to check on Dad.' She nodded regally at Officer Bledsoe. 'Thank you for your good work.'

Crystal popped up, looking appreciative. 'Yes. Very glad you know what happened. We will all feel a lot safer.'

'Has she been arrested?' Dwight Douglas stood, too, ready to follow his wife.

Officer Bledsoe picked up her laptop. 'The acting chief is careful to gather all the facts. The investigation is still continuing.'

Continuing, and the circle drawing ever closer to Fran. I desperately needed to know more.

*   *   *

The painting caught my breath, vivid red streaks tinged with gold, a swirl of purple.

I wasn't surprised that Travis Roberts ignored the ripple of the beaded door, my presence at his elbow. 'Love?'

He jerked to give me a quick stare. 'You see it.'

Oh yes, I did.

He was breathing fast. 'So get out. I'm almost there. Get out.'

I didn't budge. 'I have to know. What time did you hear that door close?'

It was as if he stood in a fog. 'Door?'

'The red door on the Chandler terrace'

'Oh hell,' he exploded. 'I don't know. Some time after eight. Maybe ten minutes, Maybe fifteen. Now get out.' Shouted.

Jennifer's pale blue Nissan was parked in a slot next to the Bide-A-Wee Bed and Breakfast, which was only a half-dozen blocks from Fran's bungalow.

Jennifer watched TV in an upstairs kitschy bedroom with doilies on the furniture, a pink chenille spread on the iron bedstead, and white French provincial furniture. On the screen, a young woman with improbable red hair (I know red hair) ran, arms wide, into the embrace of a tall, darkly handsome man. 'Ohhh,' sighed Jennifer.

The hall outside her door was quiet. I Appeared in Detective M. Loy's modest suit, gave a soft rap.

'Coming.' She opened the door, gasped, tried to shut it but I was in the doorway. I smiled. 'Just a quick visit, Mrs Roberts. A little confirmation.'

Slowly she backed up. Her eyes were shiny from the romantic scene on the screen. Her soft brown hair framed her face. A long blue angora sweater hung loose over slim black leggings. She was barefoot.

I closed the door softly behind me, maintained an encouraging smile. I gestured at a chintz-covered chair for her, sat in a blue easy chair opposite her. 'We now know what occurred on the terrace of the Chandler home last night.'

Her voice had a rote quality, 'I was at home all night. My head hurt.' She would simply repeat the words over and over again with childlike faith that if she clung to her claim, no one could prove otherwise. 'I was at—'

I interrupted. 'Now, now, you don't have to be frightened. You and your husband are cleared of any connection with the death (a much nicer word than murder) of Mrs Chandler. (And almost true. I'd seen Travis angry several times now and I was unscathed.) Of course, your testimony may be helpful at some point so I'll just be sure I have the facts correctly.'

Wide blue eyes. Her lips parted.

I spoke quickly to forestall her response. 'You, your husband and his sister, Mrs Loring, were in your living room after dinner.'

'I fixed lasagna.' A high voice. 'Travis loves lasagna.'

I beamed at her. 'Especially your lasagna, I'm sure. Your husband called Mrs Chandler at shortly after eight o'clock. He wanted to discuss his idea for a poster for the art festival. He wasn't pleased with Mrs Chandler's plans to feature a Dallas artist.'

Jennifer sat still as a hunted mouse. Not pleased was a gentle description of Travis's fury. 'Mrs Chandler hung up on him and he left to go and talk to her.' Travis stormed out. 'He drove his car midway up the hill, parked, took the path through the woods to the stairs. He hurried up to the terrace. Light streamed from the library windows. He was surprised to see the library door open. He went inside, called for Mrs Chandler. When there was no answer he strode in,' likely still in a hot fury, 'and found her dead on the sofa by the fireplace.'

For an instant she looked at me directly, sharply. 'Travis found her dead?' Her lips trembled. 'Travis found her dead.' Her voice lifted in relief. 'He didn't—' She broke off. 'He found her dead.' Tears slid down her cheeks. 'Oh. Poor Travis. Oh. How awful.'

'Very distressing for him. Of course,' a shake of my head, 'he should have called the police, but it is much better that he didn't call.'

'Better?' Her gaze was sharp, intense, not the least bit vague.

'When he hurried out to the terrace, he heard a door close as the murderer re-entered the house.'

'The murderer went in the house.' A slight breath. The

murderer inside and Travis running for the stairs. 'How horrid
for Travis.' Her voice shook. 'To see something so terrible
and go outside and hear a door close.' She shuddered. 'No
wonder he ran.' Her eyes flickered from side to side. 'Sometimes
when I have headaches I get confused about things and times,
but I remember everything now. I heard someone running and
then my phone chimed.'

'Phone chimed?'

'A reminder. Every night at eight fifteen I give Buddy his
tummy medicine. And my phone chimed and I heard somebody
running and then Travis came flying down the steps. I was in
the shadows by the steps. I wondered what happened. Oh, I
suppose I shouldn't have even cared. But I thought I would
go see. I double-dared myself. I took Buddy and went up the
stairs. I tied his leash to the railing, then I started across
the terrace and somehow I didn't like all that light and the
open door. I was scared. I turned and ran down the stairs and
I forgot all about Buddy. I remembered at the bottom of the
hill but he's clever and I knew he'd get tired of waiting and
wriggle out of his collar pretty soon and come home. Anyway,
I went home and my head hurt and I stayed in my room and
poor Travis kept knocking this morning but I didn't answer.
I decided I needed to get away just for a while and that's
why I'm here. I left a note for Travis to give Buddy his medicine.' She brightened. 'I can tear the note up. I can give him
his medicine tonight after all.'

She flew up from the chair, hurried to a closet, pulled out
a wheeled bag, plumped it on the spread. She threw belong-
ings in with no order or method. She'd manage in her own
confused fashion to explain to Travis that she'd just felt frightened to be so near a house where there was a murder but then
she felt so lonely without him.

I stood on the Chandler terrace and stared at the red door at
the end of the west wing. Travis came out of the library. A
door shut. Travis ran. Jennifer heard running steps and her
phone chimed at eight fifteen.

Eight fifteen.

*   *   *

The second floor of the Chandler house offered luxuriously appointed living quarters on Arthur and Sylvia's side of the house. Guests and Margaret Foster were quartered on the west side.

If possible, Arthur Chandler appeared more shrunken in the king-size bed than last evening. Arthur Chandler had been a big man. Now the arms lying atop the covers were thin, flaccid. He rested against a pillow, oxygen tubes in his nostrils. His large face was sunken, gray, his eyes closed. There was a slight rise and fall of the sheet as he breathed. The attendant sat in a straight chair next to the bed. She was plump with a cheerful face and was deeply absorbed in a book. I noticed the intriguing title, *The Geometry of Holding Hands*.

Sylvia's suite smelled of lilac perfume. The satin coverlet was untouched. Her purse lay on a malachite-topped table. An open box of truffles sat on a small table beside a chaise longue. There was every sense of comfort and ease for a mistress who would never return.

I welcomed the sense of energy when I reached the opposite side of the house. Elise Douglas gripped her cell phone, spoke in a steely staccato, '. . . today or he can eat that shipment.' She clicked off the phone, her surgically smooth face tight with irritation. She tossed her head, loose black hair rippling. She was elegant in a black silk caftan with streaks of magenta, flared black trousers, and black heels with magenta trim. 'I can't leave the store for a minute without everything going wrong.'

The bird in the cage behind her ruffled his feathers, cawed.

Her husband's large frame filled a leather easy chair that looked out of place in a pink-and-white room, likely her room from girlhood. He stared down at his iPad, made no response to her declaration. He tapped the iPad. 'Button Down Boy is favored Saturday. I believe in that horse and now' – the word was as exultant as if he stood on a mountaintop – 'I can buy him.' His hard face was triumphant. 'God, I can't wait. I've got a call in to the stables. He has a real shot at the Derby.'

Perhaps it was as well that he did not look toward his wife. Though her smooth face remained unchanged there was a flicker of dark fear in her eyes.

The bird cawed.

He looked up. The bird's head was cocked as if watching. Dwight gave a bark of laughter. 'Yeah, Sebastian. Now I can get that horse.'

In the hallway, I was thoughtful. Elise spoke to the lawyer Tuesday, discovered everything would belong to Sylvia for her lifetime when Arthur Chandler died. I never doubted she came back from that visit furious and upset, informed her husband. I didn't know what high dollar colts cost but likely more than even a successful businessman could afford. But now, Dwight had a call in to purchase Button Down Boy.

Stuart's bedroom was unmistakable even though he wasn't there. Perhaps he still sat in the comfortable leather retreat, a glass of whisky on the table, a cell phone in his hand. His bed wasn't made. The covers were tossed every which way. A restless night. There was a scent of whisky and pizza. A Domino's box was tossed into a wastebasket.

Stuart Chandler's bedroom was the lair of a sad man. What burdens did he carry? And were they burdens that seven mllion dollars would ease?

Crystal Pace watched a huge wall TV, muscles tensed as the stocky woman arched to serve the ball. Her opponent lunged, missed. 'Oh God, she has a no-return serve.' Crystal's eyes glowed with admiration.

Jason continued his push-ups, grunted. 'Still winning. After all these years.'

'Serena Williams,' Crystal proclaimed, 'is the greatest woman tennis player ever. Ever!'

Crystal tensed. Another serve. Game Set Match. Crystal clicked off the TV. 'Watching the replays is the only thing that's keeping me sane here.' She stood, slim and athletic in peach tennis warmups. 'God, how I miss the games. If I don't get home pretty soon, Priscilla Smith will win more games and I've held the record at the club for three years. I've got to get home.'

Jason popped to his feet. 'Yeah. It's the pits. But that cooking show you like comes on pretty soon. Yesterday that little dude fixed scallops. Those scallops looked good. How about you ask Mrs Collins to rustle up some scallops?'

'Scallops.' She nodded approval. 'Very healthy.'

'And lots of tartar sauce.'

Her husband was near the open door to a balcony, doing a series of stretches. The delicate song of wind chimes was an odd contrast to his intense exercise. His face was flushed. He glanced at his wrist. 'Almost 12,000 steps already.'

Were Crystal and Jason as untroubled as they seemed? Perhaps a few cogent questions might pierce their equanimity.

In Margaret Foster's suite at the end of the hallway, I admired pale green walls that evoked a forest glen, gold drapes. The furnishings held no hint of medieval Spain, lots of chintz and flowery upholstery. Books lay open on end tables. More books filled two white bookcases. Plastic frames held photographs of Elise, Crystal and Stuart from babyhood through college. Edward Hopper prints hung on one wall. In the bedroom, all was neat, the bed made, only a silver-backed brush and comb on the vanity.

Last night Margaret Foster needed to pull herself up the steps to the second floor, one hand over another on the banister. Did that effort reflect a woman struggling with shocking circumstances or a woman who knew more than she ever wanted to reveal?

I stood on the library side of the house, confident no one would be looking out a window. An evergreen screened me from the street. I Appeared in my modest black suit, resisted the urge to add a crimson scarf, settled for beige. I walked briskly to the front porch, punched the bell.

The cook – I suppose actually she was the Chandler housekeeper – opened the door.

'Detective M. Loy. I'm expected.' I started forward.

She automatically moved back.

'I will speak to Mrs Foster in her office. I know the way.' I moved past her, walked briskly across the marble floor into the huge gloomy living area, turned toward the hallway. The double doors were open. I walked into the hall, stopped at the door to Margaret's office, knocked twice.

'Come in.'

I stepped inside, held out my identification. 'Detective M. Loy. Some questions about last night.' My tone was bland, matter-of-fact.

Margaret Foster was a presence behind the desk, a woman comfortable in her milieu. The dark eyes beneath black brows were observant. She took my measure and I felt I was approved. She looked fully capable of deploying a battalion if that became her task. She turned a hand toward the chair in front of her desk.

I took a seat. 'You were Arthur and Sylvia Chandler's executive secretary?'

'I am the executive secretary for Chandler Exploration.' Am was emphasized.

'As I understand it, Mrs Chandler was in charge of the company since he became ill.'

'Definitely.' She leaned forward. 'This is a nightmare. I know someone attacked Sylvia, killed her, but it's unbelievable.' She pointed at me. 'Sylvia sat there. Yesterday afternoon. She always made quick decisions. She'd changed her mind about a business deal and I'm working on the e-mail.'

A decision made yesterday. 'Tell me about the change.'

She looked puzzled, but replied readily. 'She decided against selling the company.'

'I spoke earlier today to Mr Vinson. He said the deal was definite. What happened?'

Margaret looked thoughtful. 'Sylvia had an uncanny knack for looking ahead. She said she thought oil prices would go up – she was always right on top of the market – and the sale would be bigger next spring.'

'Did she consult the family?'

A quick head-shake. 'She ran the company.'

'She made a notation in her daybook.' I paraphrased it. 'She thought there was something going on with the family at dinner Tuesday night, a sense of stress. I understand Mrs Douglas discovered Tuesday that Sylvia Chandler would be in sole control of the estate upon Arthur Chandler's death.'

Margaret's eyes widened. 'Sylvia received the entire estate?' Her surprise was evident. Absently, she picked up a pencil, held it between thumb and forefinger, lightly tapped the desktop.

'A life interest.'

'Oh.' A little word but freighted with dismay. 'I didn't know. Oh.' A distant gaze, several taps with the pencil.

She was intelligent. It was easy to connect these dots. Sylvia alive meant the children and spouses had no access to wealth for perhaps twenty or thirty years. Sylvia dead meant immediate riches to each heir.

'Dinner Tuesday night,' I repeated.

She took a moment. She would not reply carelessly. 'I can't speak to Sylvia's concern. I was unaware of any strain.'

'You assumed the Chandler children would inherit at least half the estate upon his death. Are you knowledgeable about their finances?'

She leaned back in her chair, shook her head. 'No.' A frown. 'Why are you asking about their finances?'

I gave her a steady gaze. 'Sylvia Chandler's death made them all very, very rich. Now.'

Margaret spoke quickly, forcefully. 'Last night the police said the murderer came from outside.' The pencil tapped.

'We have new information.' I didn't give her time to ask. 'Please tell me about Sylvia Chandler.'

'As executive assistant I kept her informed—'

'I'm sure you performed your duties admirably. I want to know your personal opinion of Mrs Chandler.'

She spoke slowly, 'It's odd to try and describe someone you've known for years. And admired.' There was a little quiver in the words. A deep breath. 'Sylvia was an interesting mixture of qualities. She seemed to carry brightness with her. I think that was her attraction to Arthur. Almost flamboyant. She was decisive, active, engaged in the community.'

'How did Arthur's children feel about her?'

A calm reply. 'They were on good terms with her so far as I know.' She almost managed a smile.

'Did you like her?'

She nodded. 'I worked well with her.'

'Did you have an affair with Arthur Chandler?'

Her strong face abruptly hardened. 'That question is offensive.'

'Did you?'

She spoke forcefully, the words clipped, the pencil tapping a tattoo. 'I have been Arthur's executive assistant for almost thirty years. I admired him. He was one of my husband's closest friends. John and I considered Arthur and Ellen and their children as family. After John died, they invited me to live with them for awhile and somehow time passed and I've stayed. It's been a good home.'

I had a quick sense that this last was utterly genuine. I dismissed the idea that she was a spurned lover, displaced by Sylvia Chandler. Had that been the case, most surely she would not have remained a part of the family. Margaret's voice when she spoke of Arthur and Ellen and the children was for the first time soft and caring.

She seemed to realize her formality had been breached. 'I know I speak for the family,' her tone was brisk, 'in wishing you success in concluding the investigation. I understand the murderer escaped on to the terrace. The back door was wide open when Travis and I entered the library last night. Can you bring me up to date on what progress has been made?'

Her adept recasting of our interchange impressed me. Perhaps it was my turn to impress her.

'Where were you,' my tone bristled with threat, 'at precisely fifteen minutes after eight last night?' That was the moment when Travis Roberts ran, after the red door closed on the other side of the terrace.

Alarm flared in her eyes, quickly masked by a slight cough. 'Eight fifteen.' Her tone was musing. The pencil rapped several times as she thought. 'I suppose I was still here. In my office. I wasn't paying attention to the time. I finished up here, went upstairs. That was probably around eight thirty. The doorbell rang at twenty to nine. I happened to glance at the clock. I thought it was rather late for a caller. I went down and let in the young artist. He said he was bringing a painting to Mrs Chandler.'

I kept the focus on her. 'What kept you so late in your office?'

She waved a hand at an empty in-box. 'Filing. Nothing important. Simply tidying up.'

'What time did you come to your office?'

Her answer was vague. 'I don't know. After dinner I started to read a book and I remembered the filing and came down.'

'Who did you see in the hall?'

She looked surprised. 'Upstairs?'

I gestured. 'This hall. Near the pool.' She was in this area when that door to the terrace opened and someone entered.

'My door was closed. I saw no one in the hall either when I arrived or left my office.'

I wasn't interested in those times. Only eight fifteen mattered.

I rose, thanked her. I carefully closed the door behind me as I stepped into the hall. A quick glance about. I disappeared.

Margaret was still at her desk. Her unguarded face was tense. She held a cell phone, talked fast, the pencil tapping. 'A police detective is asking all about the family, everyone's finances, said you learned on Tuesday that no one would inherit anything as long as Sylvia was alive. I thought you'd want to know.' A pause. 'Of course.' She clicked off the phone, placed it on the desk.

Elise stood near the bird cage, the cell phone in one hand. She tapped a Favorite. 'Crystal, the police know Sylvia had a life interest in the estate. Now listen to me. You don't know anything about the estate, never gave it a thought. Tell Jason. Both of you look blank. The estate? Why, you don't even want to think about it with Dad dying. Remember, you don't know Sylvia had a life interest.' It was as if she pummeled her sister with the words. 'You don't know anything about a life interest. Ask what that means. Give them a puzzled stare. You Do Not Know Sylvia Had a Life Interest.' She clicked off, tapped again. 'Stu . . .'

When she clicked off, Dwight's hard face was alert. 'Looks like the hounds are starting to sniff around. As for us,' he spoke lazily but his gaze was intense, 'you never mentioned the estate to me, had almost forgotten about it with everything that's happened.'

Elise lifted her eyes, looked at him. 'So you don't know either?'

He turned over a big hand. 'Nope. You didn't bother to mention it because you dismissed it from your mind. You didn't think it was worth discussing.' Now a wolfish grin. 'And the cops can't prove differently.'

'So I'm the only one who knew?'

He locked eyes with her. 'Right.'

Elise turned away. Her tightly planed face looked old, old and frightened.

Somehow it didn't surprise me that Dwight was willing to throw his wife under the bus. I returned to the hall, Appeared, knocked.

Dwight opened the door. He was a very big man. I looked up, waved my leather ID folder. 'Detective M. Loy. I have some questions in regard to Mrs Chandler.'

He remained in the doorway, took the folder, looked at it carefully. I wasn't concerned. The Department of Good Intentions is punctilious in details.

He handed the folder back, turned to his wife. 'A detective, Elise.' He dropped into the big leather chair in his usual sprawl. 'We have a few minutes.'

I sat in a small chair opposite the sofa. The afternoon sun spilled across the room, turning the magenta streaks on Elise's tunic into flame, revealing the fine surgical lines on her too-smooth face. The sunlight touched Sebastian's cage and his black feathers gleamed.

Dwight's gaze was demanding. 'What's the status of the woman on the terrace?'

Elise was brisk. 'She owns a shop. Do you suppose Sylvia owed her money?'

Dwight gave a bay of laughter. 'More likely the woman owed Sylvia.'

'Mrs Loring has been interviewed. We are discovering more about Mrs Chandler's last week. Mrs Chandler felt uncomfortable at dinner Tuesday evening.'

Elise's shoulders tightened. As if realizing the revealing change in posture, she reached up, massaged her neck. 'A sore neck. I get them sometimes.'

'Stress can do that,' I observed. 'I suppose you haven't slept well since Tuesday.'

Now she was on full alert. Likely knowing where the conversation was headed.

Dwight still sprawled but his deep voice boomed. 'You got that wrong, Detective. Elise sleeps like a log.'

I was quick. 'Even though Mr Vinson informed her that Sylvia Chandler scooped up the entire estate upon her husband's death?'

Dwight sat bolt upright, swung to stare at his wife. 'Elise, what's that all about?'

Elise's voice was thin but steady. 'Oh, I meant to mention it to you, Dwight. But I was having all that trouble with shipments and I forgot.'

Dwight looked satisfied.

I was sharp. 'You forgot to mention that you and your brother and sister would not have access to any portion of the estate if Sylvia outlived your father?'

Elise fluttered long lashes. 'I make it a practice not to worry about things I can't change. So I forgot all about it.' Her dark eyes defied me.

She would lie. He would lie. They would all lie. But I knew she knew and I knew Crystal and Stuart knew.

'On Tuesday,' I spaced each word, 'you learned that no portion of the estate would come to any of you if Sylvia outlived your father. Sylvia is brutally killed Friday night.'

Silence. Elise stared at me with dark, empty eyes. Dwight looked big and comfortable sprawled in the chair.

'Sylvia is murdered and your payoff is seven million dollars.'

Neither responded.

I was determined to shake their complacency. 'We will expect financial statements from each of you, the status of your companies, indebtedness, notes due.'

She drew a quick breath. Alarm flared in Dwight's eyes. I never doubted they were up against a wall financially. One advantage to conducting an investigation according to my own rules is I never worry whether what I do is proper. Could the police demand that information? I neither knew nor cared. I'd achieved what I intended. I now knew they had financial pressures and the specter of inheritance delayed for a woman's lifetime was a mighty motive to shorten that lifetime.

Elise fluttered a long hand. 'After all, I wasn't worried about the future. Sylvia was always generous.'

Dwight gave his wife an admiring nod.

Sebastian cocked his head, cawed.

I folded a losing hand and dealt new cards. 'The investigation will easily document that seven million dollars will accrue to each heir as a result of Mrs Chandler's murder. As to the night of her murder,' my tone was matter of fact, as if it were a perfunctory question, 'Mrs Douglas, where were you at eight fifteen?'

Her expression never changed. Perhaps it was the surgeon's work or perhaps she had no guilty knowledge. She responded quickly, 'Here, of course. Dwight and I came upstairs after dinner and didn't go down until we heard sirens.'

I looked at Dwight.

He remained in his sprawl, drawled, 'Not too much shaking around here at night. If we'd known somebody was going to burst in off the terrace and attack Sylvia, we could have rushed down and yelled boo out the terrace door.'

The bird cawed.

I stood. 'I'll be in touch.' My tone indicated I wasn't amused. I was at the door when he spoke again.

'Why eight fifteen?'

I turned. 'Information received. Did you hear or see anything at eight fifteen?'

Elise trilled. 'I was telling Dwight about my idea for a spring show.'

He ignored his wife. His pale green eyes moved to the window.

I looked out the window. Bare branches wavered in a breeze.

His gaze slid back to me. 'Information received. What does that mean?'

Sebastian cawed.

'An informant.' On that, I opened the door and stepped into the hall. I shut the door quickly. I disappeared.

In their sitting room, Elise held her cell, talked fast. 'Crystal, the detective's nosing around about money. Remember what I told you. You know nothing about Dad's estate. Nothing. And you think it's sickening to talk about money when Sylvia's dead and Dad is dying. That's all you have to say . . . We can talk later.' She tapped end. 'I thought I'd better tell her again. Crystal blurts things out. She's always super confident. She's won too many tennis games.'

Dwight looked as if he was thinking hard.

Elise frowned. 'I think everything will be all right.'

Dwight roused from his reverie, raised a dark brow. 'The cops have to go through the motions.' Then he grinned. 'Hey, I didn't know you needed an alibi.'

She looked shocked. 'What are you talking about?'

'You were pretty quick to say we were up here at eight fifteen.'

She relaxed in her chair. 'Why not? It was just a little past that when you came up from the pool.' The bird moved on his perch, cawed.

'Right. Just a little after that.' Those pale green eyes moved back to the window.

The big black bird cawed.

Crystal held her cell phone, her chiseled features tight, looked at Jason. 'I don't want to talk to that detective.' She stood by the open door to a balcony. A distant ring of wind chimes floated into the room.

'Piece of cake, honey. Just give her a blank look, say you don't know a thing about money, you leave all that up to your husband.'

'Up to you? That's what I did.' Her tone was grim. 'You and money and gambling. I can't believe you went through your money and mine, mortgaged the house. Nothing left in the bank. How could you?'

He no longer looked like an aging preppie. He looked depleted, diminished, like an old man. 'I had to pay up. You don't understand, Crystal. What they do to you if you don't pay up. Look, I won't go back to the casino anymore. I promise.'

'Won't you? Can I believe you? I don't know what we would have done if Sylvia hadn't—'

He broke in. 'Don't say things like that. Don't think them. Look, just tell the detective we have plenty of money, never have to worry about money.'

'Plenty of money. Now.'

Arthur Chandler was dying. Seven million dollars could likely support even the most profligate of gamblers. And I was quite sure a Missouri Valley tennis champion would limit Jason's access to future funds.

He was urgent. 'This is no time to rehash all that. When the detective comes, you don't know anything about the estate, and we have plenty of money.'

In the hall outside their door, I Appeared and knocked. The door opened and I went through my routine, presented ID, mentioned a few questions.

Crystal waved a hand at a narrow bench, sat on a small sofa, gestured to her husband to join her. The breeze from the open balcony door stirred her blonde hair and the sound of wind chimes wafted cheerfully inside.

When I was settled on the rather uncomfortable bench and faced them, Jason spread manicured fingernails on the knees of his sweatpants. 'Hey, I like *CSI*. Fun stuff. Have you found the guy who killed Sylvia?'

'Guy?'

'You know, whoever came in from the backyard.' He leaned forward, looked hopeful, perhaps expecting a report of foot-prints and bloodhounds and a bearded stranger manacled in a patrol car. Jason appeared relaxed but he looked quickly several times at his wife, likely to bolster her, keep her calm, keep her quiet. Despite her stiff exchange with Jason about their finances, Crystal appeared composed, her well-exercised body relaxed. Their performances reminded me it is unwise to underestimate anyone. As Mama always told us kids, 'Everyone wears a party face on the outside. Remember everyone has an inside.'

I lowered the boom. 'Your sister informed you last Tuesday

that there would be no inheritance after your father's death, that Sylvia would control the estate for her lifetime.'

Crystal's blue eyes never wavered. 'I'm afraid you are mistaken. My sister and I have never discussed the estate. Neither of us is thinking about money at a time like this.' Her voice was low. 'Our father is dying. That's what concerns us.'

Jason rolled his shoulders. 'Somebody steered you wrong. Crystal would have told me and,' his voice was smooth, 'she didn't.'

'Interesting. It's our understanding that Mrs Douglas informed her sister and brother about the shocking news that Sylvia would control the estate.'

Crystal toyed with the zipper on her warmup jacket. 'No.'

Jason was relaxed, too. 'There's been some mistake. We didn't know anything about the estate. Right, Crystal?'

She was firm. 'We don't know anything about the estate. That can wait until Dad is gone.'

I gave each of them a cynical, doubting look, stood. 'We'll be getting financial statements. Debts. Bank accounts.' A prosecutor would have no trouble establishing a motive for Crystal and Jason.

I let them sit in stiff silence. Both faced desolation if Sylvia lived. Crystal might lose her home, see her social status destroyed; perhaps, most devastatingly, be stripped of her country club membership and the tennis she loved. As for Jason, he knew what happened to gamblers who didn't pay their debts.

I pointed at Crystal, barked, 'Last night.'

She was alert, stared with an unwavering look. The wind chimes were an odd contrast to her tense posture.

Staccato demand. 'Where were you at eight fifteen?'

She gestured toward a desktop with a laptop and keyboard. 'I was working on my introduction. I'm president of the Women's Tennis League and I will introduce Serena Williams when she speaks at the club next month.' She spoke the athlete's name in a tone of awe.

I looked at Jason. 'Where were you at eight fifteen?'

'Playing pinball downstairs.' He made squeezing motions with both hands. 'I did great.'

I maintained a grim expression as I stood, took my leave. When the door closed behind me, I disappeared.

Crystal stood on her feet. 'That awful woman. She knows we're broke. And if Sylvia—'

'Don't say that. Not to me. Not to anyone.'

Laptop and pinball. So neither had an alibi. And they were backs-against-a-wall broke.

Stuart stood by the window in his room. He held a cell to his ear. His round face puckered. '. . . answer, Melissa. Please.' He waited a moment, took a breath, 'Melissa, please don't delete my message. Things have changed. I'm not going to be broke. We can go to Bermuda. Like we did on our honeymoon. Please call me. Please.' There was a prayer and a plea in his voice. 'I won't drink anymore. That was because I lost my job and I couldn't find one and everything was rotten. But if you give me another chance, I promise. Oh God, yes, I promise. Please.' He clicked off.

He stared down at the phone, tears in his eyes. 'I promise, Melissa. I promise. No more booze. God, I don't know if I can . . . Yeah. I can. I will.'

It took a moment for Stuart to answer his door. He managed to look presentable this morning, eyes clear, hair combed, and a polo shirt and khakis instead of worn sweats.

I showed the ID. 'A few questions.'

He held the door wide for me, appeared welcoming, eager. 'Have you made progress?' He waited for me to sit before dropping into an easy chair.

'The investigation has uncovered a great many facts concerning the financial status of you and your sisters and their spouses.'

His eyes blinked and his face creased in a frown.

I was pleasant. 'What is your permanent address, Mr Chandler?'

He moved uncomfortably. 'I don't have one right now.'

'Can you explain?'

A breath. 'I've been taking some time off, doing a little traveling.' He looked away from me.

'Where are you employed?'

He stared at the floor, mumbled. 'I'm not working right now.'

'Where did you work?'

'Spartacus Advertising.' His voice was dull.

'You left there when?'

'Two weeks ago.'

'Were you fired?'

He lifted his gaze, the eyes of a hurt puppy. He didn't want to answer, knew the truth would be easily discovered, muttered, 'Yes.'

'What income do you have?'

He shook his head again.

'On Tuesday,' I made each word distinct, 'your sister learned that none of you would inherit a penny as long as Sylvia was alive.'

He lifted his gaze, stared at me hopelessly. 'No.'

'Are you claiming you didn't know that Sylvia held a life interest in the estate?'

Elise warned him, but he didn't pretend ignorance. Instead, his round face, a face that liked to smile, twisted in protest. 'Don't talk like that. None of us would hurt Sylvia. Not my sisters. Not their husbands. Not me. Don't talk like that.'

'It's interesting what people say, what their words reveal. You understand what I am saying. Each one of you is desperate for money and each one of you will never have to worry again about money. Because Sylvia died. Those words are harsh. They are true. And I want to know about your own words last night, Mr Chandler.'

'I don't remember much about last night. I had too much to drink. God knows what I said.'

'You spoke quite lucidly, Mr Chandler. Tell me what you meant when you said, "In the nick of time, but that's a crime."'

He said stubbornly, 'I don't remember last night. It's all a blur.'

'When Sylvia died, your money troubles ended. Within a few days or a week you will be master of seven million dollars. So she died in the nick of time, didn't she?'

He stared straight ahead, his eyes haunted.

'Mr Chandler,' my tone was stern, 'exactly where were you at eight fifteen last night?'

He creased his face as if thinking, 'Eight fifteen. Yeah. I was in the dart room. I went down there right after dinner. A good bar. Darts to throw. I was there until I heard a siren.'

I studied his face, his haunted face. Death was in the room with us, Sylvia's death and the truth that he and his sisters and their spouses all needed for Sylvia to die before Arthur.

I took a last look at the terrace. The red door on the west side was closed, but last night a murderer slipped inside to safety. The late afternoon wind and lowering sky matched my mood. I'd spoken to all the residents. Margaret was obviously stressed. Did she think one of the family was a murderer? Elise was quick to claim an alibi. Dwight observed her with cool green eyes. What did he see? Jobless Stuart hoped a grand holiday would save his marriage and now he would have the money to plan that trip. Crystal and Jason were pampered creatures. Their life of ease and comfort faced extinction.

In the nick of time . . .

EIGHT

S am's office was a warm refuge from the chill of the terrace. I turned on the lights. The thermostat was still set at 72. I hurried to his desk, slipped into the chair, tapped his computer, checked e-mail.

I found the report I sought, factual, matter-of-fact, but to me the words loomed as large as the iconic sign on the famous hill above Hollywood. I clapped my hands together. Oh yes. Yes. Yes. Yes.

The cat lifted her head, looked at me curiously. I arrived eager to share my news, but Fran wasn't home. The cat turned away from me, walked past me as a car door slammed. I looked out the window.

Fran stood beside Don's red Corvette, hands on the sill of the door. The wind tousled her golden ringlets, tugged at her navy-blue cardigan. 'Thank you. Thank you for a perfect day.'

The car remained in place as Fran came up the walk. On the porch she turned and smiled and waved. She stepped inside and closed the door and only then did a deep rumble sound as Don drove away. She was smiling as she took two steps and scooped up the black cat. She buried her face in Muff's neck for a moment then lifted her head and began to sing, 'Oh What a Beautiful Day!' Oklahomans know and love the song which opens the musical *Oklahoma!* Her alto voice was rich and strong and she curved into a slow dance step, holding Muff.

I am a robust soprano and I know all the lyrics. I joined in on the second verse.

Fran stopped for an instant, her head jerking as she searched for her duet partner. Muff squirmed free and dropped to the floor.

I came near and reached out to grasp Fran's hands in mine. I tugged. 'Let's dance.' After only an instant's resistance, she joined in the lyrics and we made a high stepping circle in the small foyer. We finished, laughing and breathless.

I dropped her hands and clapped.

Fran clapped in response. 'Today who cares if I'm nuts? It doesn't matter. Why not a duet? I've had the most beautiful day and I'm happy and it's a long time since I've been happy.'

'I'm happy, too.' To celebrate, I Appeared in a gorgeous sea-blue short-sleeve jersey knit dress accented with multi-colored swirls. 'We sing well together.'

She tilted her head, studied me. 'I remember your hair. That's just how I imagined it before. Red like a splash of sunset. Everything's hazy in my mind about last night. I thought I imagined you because I was upset. Now I'm happy and I see you. Go figure. But anyway, here you are again.' She gave an approving nod. 'Nice dress. I have to hand it to my imagin-ation. If I'm going to hang out with a figment, why not a good-looking redhead in a knockout dress?'

I grinned, 'Flattery will get you a gold star.'

'Gold star? I remember the first time I took home a report card with a gold star. My mom made brownies and she put buttercream stars on each brownie. After that, we always made them for special occasions and called them Gold Star Brownies.'

I walked near, tapped her shoulder. 'By the way, I'm not a figment.'

She slowly reached out, touched my arm. Her fingers brushed my cheek.

Colors swirled. I disappeared.

She stood rigid, eyes darting around the entryway.

'I'm still here.' Colors swirled. This time I chose an emerald-green cardigan, white blouse, gray wool slacks and gray leather loafers.

She covered her face with her hands, slowly spread her fingers wide, peeked. 'I liked the dress better.' Her hands fell. 'I give up. I'm either so crazy I can imagine warm flesh under my fingers or you are who you say you are.' She gazed into my eyes. 'If you're here, Great-Aunt Hortense gets the last laugh.' Fran pressed fingertips to each temple. 'OK, when my boots floated in the kitchen I thought you were part of a crazy night. And then you insisted you were here from Heaven.'

Her hands dropped and she clasped them together so tightly the skin blanched. 'So I guess you are real and I'm in big trouble. Today when Don and I were driving and laughing, I thought last night was behind me. But here you are. It's like Dracula's at the door and you're the welcome committee. Come right in. Lucky me. You're the stamp that says File Closed, Fran Loring's on her way to jail.'

I was chagrined to see happiness drain away like champagne from a carelessly tipped flute, leaving emptiness behind. The glow of her day was replaced by dread. I rushed to reassure her. 'I'm not the welcome committee for Dracula or a File Closed stamp. I have good news. That's why I'm here. I've going to find the murderer. I'm very close.' Well, perhaps very close was an exaggeration. 'I have proof,' great emphasis, 'that the murderer is a resident of the Chandler house. Last night the murderer was on the far side of the terrace when Travis arrived.'

Fran's eyes widened in horror. 'The murderer saw him?'

'The murderer watched to see what he would do, but Travis didn't raise an alarm.'

Fran was frantic. 'We have to find Travis, protect him.'

His big sister still wanted the best for gifted, difficult Travis.

'There's no danger to Travis. The murderer by now is sure Travis didn't see anyone. The murderer was in dark shadows near a door that opens into the hallway by the pool and exercise rooms. Imagine for a moment that you killed Sylvia Chandler. You slipped outside, leaving the door open, and hurried across the terrace. Suddenly you hear footsteps. Travis is clearly visible in the light streaming from the library windows. He goes inside. You wait to see if he reports Sylvia's death. You take one step, another, reach the door into the house. Travis bolts outside. He gazes frantically around the terrace. You are safe in the shadows but he must not see you. Quickly you grab the knob, open the door. As you step inside you use a scarf or a handkerchief to wipe the doorknob. Once inside,' I spaced the words, 'you . . . close . . . the . . . door. Now you are free and safe in the house.'

Fran scarcely breathed.

'Travis hears the door shut and he runs.'

Fran shivered. 'If Travis had arrived any sooner . . .' She briefly closed her eyes, opened them. 'The door shut.'

'Before you reached the terrace.'

She gave me a weary smile. 'The police won't believe him. Even if they did, they would dismiss the shutting of a door, say that doesn't mean the person who killed Sylvia shut the door.'

'The person who entered took time to polish the doorknobs, inside and out. There's the proof.'

'I don't think so. Maybe someone else found her and didn't want to call the police and polished the knobs.'

'Not enough time. Sylvia was alive when Travis called her. He arrives within ten minutes and she is dead. There simply wasn't time for anyone else to have entered and left the library but the person who killed her. And,' I was on a roll, 'why was the door to the pool hallway unlocked? I'm sure the door is normally locked, only open if someone chooses to go out on the terrace that way and return. Someone unlocked that door, came outside. Was it a lovely night for a walk?' I remembered the sharp cold wind. 'A resident of the Chandler house came out on to the terrace with the sole purpose of entering the library, killing Sylvia, and returning. I am positive that's what happened because the outside doorknob and the inside door-knob have no trace of fingerprints. No trace. Shiny clean. Not even a smudge. Those doorknobs were wiped very carefully.' I took a victory lap. 'I cleverly' – surely it is proper to take pride in an important achievement – 'arranged for the police to fingerprint the inner and outer doorknobs of the door. No fingerprints. Ta Da. Trumpet tattoo. And I came to tell you.' I beamed at her.

She did not beam in return. 'So a couple of doorknobs don't have any fingerprints. That proves somebody in the house killed Sylvia?'

I tugged at her elbow, maneuvered her to the front door. 'Open it.'

I punched the words like Rosie the Riveter on an airplane wing.

She grabbed the knob, yanked open the door.

I tapped the hand holding the knob. 'Fingerprints.' I yanked off her hand, lifted the hem of my cardigan, swiped at the knob. 'The only way the knob on any door can be absolutely totally without a trace of even a smudge is that someone wiped them clean. Both the outer and inner knobs on the red door are as shiny as the day they rolled on a conveyor belt at the factory to be packed. So get your happy face back. The murderer entered the Chandler house and I'm headed back there right now.'

But a whiff of coal smoke took me to Sam's office instead.

To my surprise, Wiggins Appeared on Sam's sofa before I could say a word. His stiff cap was tipped back on his russet hair. His broad face was kindly.

I Appeared in a pale blue sweater set and a tweed skirt, gray flats. Understated. I joined him on the sofa. 'No fingerprints is huge.'

He was admiring. 'You are making grand progress. As soon as the acting chief is apprised of the door handles with no fingerprints, our Fran will be safe. In fact, you could hop aboard the Express now.'

Coal smoke thickened

I wasn't confident Howie Harris would agree. 'Wiggins, it is imperative that I remain until Fran is officially cleared. You know how important it is to be sure of the outcome.'

'Oh. Perhaps you are right. But you've accomplished enough work for today. I'm especially pleased that your most important task is right on track.'

'My most important task?'

He nodded happily. 'So now you can take the evening off. Settle in at a nice room at Rose Bower and tomorrow no doubt all will be clear to the police.'

Rose Bower is the Italianate mansion left to Goddard College by the Marlow family. Wiggins is especially fond of Rose Bower because his beloved Lorraine Marlow lived there for so many years.

Coal smoke swirled. 'Perhaps stay in The Gusher Room.' The second floor of Rose Bower is devoted to bedrooms for distinguished guests of the college and each room has its own name.

Wiggins's approving smile was better than any gold star.

'Keep up the good work. Don and . . .' And he was gone.

I was buoyed. I was on the right track. But my most important task? *Don and . . .*

Don was in a small study at his computer. He clicked several times. I looked over his shoulder as he skimmed several reports. He read too rapidly for me to catch more than a fact here and there: . . . *paw prints near site of boot imprints . . . estimate dog likely weighing less than 12 pounds . . . autopsy . . . well-nourished female . . . victim caught unaware . . . no self-defense . . . poker used as weapon . . . upper portion of poker scrubbed clean of fingerprints . . . room temperature at nine p.m. consistent with door to terrace open forty-five minutes . . .*

'Oh clever.' I clapped my hand over my mouth.

Don Smith's head jerked, but the study held only him and the door to the hall was closed. Finally, his broad mouth twisted in an odd grin. 'No, buddy, she's not here. Didn't sound like Fran anyway. Husky voice. Fran's voice is like a clear sweet bell. Fran . . . Come on. Buddy, focus on—'

Brrring. Doorbell held. Rapid knocks.

Don pushed back the chair, stood. He moved with the grace of an athlete. His face was set and hard. I doubted the importunate visitor was going to be welcomed. I followed him into the hall and to the front door. The bell continued to ring, a shrill accompaniment to demanding knocks.

Don checked through the peephole. He looked big, powerful, and combative. He opened the door.

Howie Harris's index finger pressed hard against the button.

Don folded his arms, looked down. 'Yeah?'

Howie jerked his hand back. 'Knew you were here.' A thumb jerked over his shoulder at the red car on the driveway. 'So what's the deal? You and the perp.'

'Did Ginger have fun in Pawhuska?'

Howie blinked. 'How'd you know?'

'Ginger kept a little too close on my tail. Tell her next time she follows a car to let another car get between occasionally.'

'That's not the point.' Howie's face reddened. 'You should have known I'd set a watch on the perp.'

'Don't call Fran Loring the perp.' Each word was as distinct as the rise and fall of a sledgehammer.

Howie sputtered, 'I could have had you stopped. I could have had you arrested. A member of the force conniving with a murderer. It doesn't get much worse than that.' His face quivered with indignation.

Don rocked back on his heels, spoke quietly. 'She's innocent, Howie. Think about it. You know why people get killed. Money. Or Sex. Sex. Or Money. This time it's money. Let me get at the people living in that house. I'll find the murderer.'

'You think you're special. Sam looked the other way when you went off on your own. This time you've gone too far. Running around with a suspect. I'm going to file an official reprimand.'

'Be my guest.' Don's drawl was unrepentant.

Howie balled his fists. 'I'm acting chief. You were up for a promotion. I'll see you don't get promoted.' Howie turned on his heel and strode toward the modest gray sedan parked behind the flamboyant red car.

It was as though a bright light beamed in a foggy tunnel. *Don and . . .* I welcomed a moment of clarity. My tasks were obvious. Clear Fran. Make sure Don gets his promotion. Wiggins was quite cavalier about Fran, apparently convinced I would prevail easily. He saw restoring Don's promotion as a greater challenge. To my mind, missing out on a promotion didn't compare with being arrested. I had no doubt which effort required my concentration. I suppose I should have been regretful about Don's promotion. Instead I was pumped. I wasn't alone in protecting Fran. Don Smith was on the case.

'Clair de Lune' played on a sound system in the marbled entrance hall. The fountain splashed softly. Silver clinked on china and voices rose and fell in the dining room visible through an archway. I sniffed. The scent of excellent beef. The voices sounded cheerful. I didn't feel at all cheerful. I'd talked to each of them today: stiff-faced Elise, her somewhat brutish husband Dwight, fumbling, bumbling-with-the-aura-of-a-loser Stu, athletic Crystal, self-absorbed Jason and somber Margaret. I'd flung out my demand, 'Where were you at eight fifteen?'

What more could I do? Detective M. Loy had no excuse to return this evening. I was here in the Chandler house but to what purpose? Was I to move from room to room, unseen, unheralded, like an ineffectual ghost wandering on a misty moor? I pushed the image away. Wiggins insists that we are emissaries. Not ghosts. Never ghosts. If I wasn't careful, coal smoke would engulf me and I'd be plumped on to a plush seat aboard the Rescue Express.

The scent of food and the chattering voices drew me into the elegant dining room. I looked down at a sumptuous buffet: rare tenderloin, grilled scallops, sweet potato casserole, steamed asparagus, a green salad with strawberries, pecans, goat cheese and avocado.

The luscious lunch at the Mercantile seemed long ago and far away. I steeled myself. I was famished, but duty first. I stood near the buffet. The diners were animated, Elise using both hands to describe the sweep of a gown, Jason tapping a large wristwatch and crowing, 'Twelve thousand steps.' Dwight managed to sit mostly upright. He downed a half-glass of red wine. Stuart looked down the table at Margaret. 'I got an idea.' He looked earnest. 'Since there's going to be plenty of money, I vote we give Mrs Collins a bonus. She's fed us like royalty for a week now and dinner tonight is the best yet.'

Elise frowned. 'Hush Stu, she'll hear you.'

'Maybe she should.'

As the siblings wrangled, I edged to the sideboard. No one was looking this way. I lifted the skirt of the tablecloth and quick as a fox in a chicken coop I piled a little bit of every-thing on a salad plate. I dropped the cloth and stepped to the end of the sideboard. I held the plate out of sight from the table and ate fast. I was taking a last bite when Dwight boomed, 'Listen up, people. We need to liven things up around here. I've watched enough Netflix and ESPN and jogged to the pond and back. Boring.' Pronounced bo-ring.

I debated what to do with the plate. I finally eased it on to the buffet. I doubted the visitors cleared. The remarkable Mrs Collins might be puzzled, but it was not hers to reason why there might be an extra plate.

I was in a much better humor when I again looked down

at the table. I wondered about dessert, noticed there wasn't a wine glass at Stuart's place.

Elise nibbled on a celery stick. Her plate showed little evidence of use. A small remnant of tenderloin, some salad and asparagus. What price thinness? 'There's always Jeopardy,' Crystal offered.

Dwight poured more wine. 'I can do you one better. I suppose that odious policewoman talked to everyone?' Elise reached for her wine glass, held it tight. The smile slid from Stuart's face. Crystal looked tense. Jason touched her arm. Margaret stiffened.

Odious? If I had a face that would be at home on a 'Wanted' poster, I wouldn't be calling other people odious.

'But,' he waited until everyone looked at him, 'she gave me an idea. She was obsessed with, "Where were you," he intoned in a deep voice, "at eight fifteen?" Here's what I want everyone to do. Take a selfie of exactly where you were at eight fifteen last night. Go wherever you were and selfie up. The person who comes up with the funniest photo will be the grand winner. Maybe I'll stand on my head in the door to the pool. Look cross-eyed. Stick out your tongue. At precisely,' deep voice again, 'eight fifteen.'

Crystal was eager. 'What do we win? I'd like tickets to the Open next year.'

Jason shouted, 'Tickets to Cabo.'

Dwight's big face pursed in thought. 'Yeah, we need a prize.'

He looked at Margaret. 'Just for the hell of it, cut a check. Maybe a hundred grand. It's worth a hundred grand to see what everyone comes up with.' He pushed back his chair. 'It gives us something to do tonight.' He paused then intoned in a deep, quavery voice, 'Eight fifteen.'

Elise laughed.

Coal smoke swirled.

NINE

I pulled out the bottom left drawer of Sam's desk, poured out a handful of M&Ms, handed the sack for Wiggins.

'It's good that there's no one here but us.' Wiggins's chuckle was robust. 'Floating candies would surely startle an observer.' M&Ms rolled from the sack into his unseen hand.

I laughed and took the bag from the air.

Wiggins Appeared, his blue cap with the black brim tilted back on his thick thatch of russet hair. His florid face was pleased. This time it was he who patted the sofa seat, inviting me to join him.

I Appeared too, back in my Detective Loy suit. I like to reassure Wiggins that I am quite a serious person despite flaming red hair and a penchant for Lulu's. No frivolity here.

'I'm most pleased, Bailey Ruth. I know you will devise a clever way to point the police in the proper direction. Eight fifteen. Yes, indeed.' He gestured at the computer. 'As soon as you use that thing' – computers were far distant from Wiggins's 1910 train station – 'and make your report to Chief Cobb, the Rescue Express will be here.'

'Eight fifteen.' I might have sounded a bit strangled.

'Eight fifteen? Oh, of course. That door closed. Clever of you. Fran is saved.'

'Wiggins,' despite their protective shell, the M&Ms felt sweaty in my hand, 'I must be at the Chandler house at eight fifteen.' Dwight's entertainment required each person to be at a precise location. One participant would be lying. I wanted to see each one where they claimed to be last night.

'Mmmmm.' A considering tone.

He popped the last M&Ms in his mouth. 'Very well. Tidy things up, Bailey Ruth and—' His brow furrowed. 'Oh. A summons. Tumbulgum. I must go.' He disappeared. Coal smoke thinned, swirled away.

* * *

A single wall sconce glowed in the huge Chandler entry hall, providing very little illumination. No music played. The fountain splashed. All was darkness to my right and left.

I'll admit I was curious to see Elise Douglas's selfie. Elise told Detective Loy that she and Dwight were together in their suite at eight fifteen the night before. Dwight asked if she needed an alibi.

Elise settled in a comfortable chair, picked up her cell phone, gave it a wide-eyed stare, tapped. She was a dramatic figure in a red silk robe emblazoned with a golden dragon. Her dark hair was piled atop her head.

Stuart's suite was empty. I found him downstairs in the dart room with the deer head and the leather sofas. Again he stared at his cell phone. The bottle of Scotch on the table was nearly empty, but it was capped and no glass sat on the end table. He pushed up from the sofa, walked to a wet bar, grabbed a glass. He returned, plopped on to the sofa, placed the glass on the table with the bottom up. His face held resolve and hope and uncertainty. He took a quick breath, grabbed the cell, clicked a selfie, slid the phone in his pocket. A pause then he picked up the bottle, slowly unscrewed the lid, held the bottle near the glass, began to tip. The bottle jerked upright. Scotch splashed on to the table. His nose wrinkled. He put the fifth down, picked up the cap with a shaking hand, jammed the cap on the bottle, slammed the bottle on the table. 'I will not. I will not. I will not.'

In the Paces' suite, Jason stood by the hall door. Crystal sat at the small desk. 'I might as well work on my introduction. Oh Jason, only three weeks and she'll be at the club. Meeting her is going to be the best thing ever.' Crystal brushed back a strand of hair. 'Thank God I've had that to work on. It's fun finding out more about Serena. And her line of clothes is just fabulous. Being cooped up here is driving me crazy. I haven't played in three weeks.' She frowned. 'I hope Genevieve is doing at least two buckets of balls with the kids every day.'

Jason did a squat lunge, returned to the doorway. 'They'll probably serve better than you when we get back.' He saw her frown. 'Hey, just kidding. Anyway, it's about time for the photos. I'd better get downstairs.'

In her office on the ground floor, Margaret gazed at the cell phone lying on her desk. Finally, with a shrug, she picked it up, turned the face toward her, tapped.

Jason crouched at the largest pinball machine, gave it an affectionate pat. He pulled out his cell, twisted to snap a photo of himself with the machine at his back. He slid the cell in a pocket, turned and gripped the levers. Flip. Flip. Flip. Lights flashed.

I opened the door to the pool. All was quiet and dark. It was perhaps a few minutes after eight fifteen. I'd missed Dwight's selfie, but I was quite sure I knew what it would show: Dwight standing on the threshold, looking up the hall at a fast-moving figure.

Fran hummed as she washed a mixing bowl, turned to place it in the dishwasher. An apple pie cooled on the counter. I sniffed. As Mama always told us kids, 'Be sweet and I'll cut you a piece.' I stood beside the counter, admired the golden-brown lattice crust. I took a breath and warbled 'Apple Pan Dowdy.'

After an initial gasp, Fran laughed. 'I made the pie for Don, but I'll give you a piece.' She gestured toward the white kitchen table.

I Appeared. I smoothed the soft sleeve of a double-breasted plaid jacket, tan stripes within blue squares, a matching blue cotton blouse, a chunky turquoise necklace, smooth-fitted cream slacks, blue flats. I appreciated the admiration in her gaze.

She joined me at the kitchen table. The pie with a dash of whipped cream was scrumptious. I felt comfortable, an interlude with a friend.

'All is well with Travis and Jennifer.'

Fran shook her head. 'Travis called this afternoon. Jennifer's walked out on him.'

'She's walking back. I told her Travis found the body and that's why he ran. I'm afraid she thought Travis lost his temper and killed Sylvia. By the time she gets home, she'll have dismissed any memory of that and tell him she just wanted to be away from the hill, why it was so scary what happened up there. And he'll tell her how great his new painting is and never question what she says.'

'How did you . . .' She broke off. 'I suppose you're everywhere. If you know everything, who killed Sylvia?'

'Someone in the Chandler house.'

She was impatient. 'That doesn't get us very far.'

I wasn't exactly miffed, but I felt Detective M. Loy deserved some credit. 'I know the murderer was on the far side of the terrace at eight fifteen. They all claim to have been in another place. Elise said she and Dwight were in the suite, but she lied. Dwight was downstairs at the pool. He goes down every night at a quarter to eight and swims for half an hour. According to their statements to me, Crystal was at a desk with her laptop, Jason was in the game room, Stuart was pouring Scotch in the dart room, and Margaret was in her office.'

Fran repeated their names. 'Don told me about them.'

I suspected she had a clear vision of each of them: stylish imperious Elise, powerful hard-faced Dwight, tennis-playing Crystal, perennial jock Jason, sensitive troubled Stuart, intelligent reliable Margaret.

'One of them lied. One of them saw Travis arrive.'

Fran's eyes widened. 'The murderer was on the terrace when Travis came?'

'The murderer watched Travis enter the library and a moment later rush out. The murderer was frantic to get inside unseen.' I imagined the panicked wiping of the outer knob, pulling the door open, stepping inside, closing the door, snapping the lock, wiping the inside lock, dashing up the hall. 'Travis heard the door close. He ran. And I'm the one—'

The cell phone lying on the counter rang.

Fran pushed back her chair. 'My work phone. Somebody probably has to have a cut-glass vase for some flowers, right now on a cold November night, and Mitchell Antiques always comes through.' She was smiling as she clicked on the phone, held it to her ear. 'Mitchell Antiques. How may I help you?'

Fran suddenly went rigid, her breaths coming fast.

TEN

Fran trembled. She drew in upon herself, as if shrinking from blows. Then she held the phone in the palm of her right hand, stared at the screen.

I was at her side, my hand on her arm. 'What's wrong?'

'An awful whisper.' Her breath came in jerks. She tapped the phone. 'Don,' her voice was a cry, the words running together, 'I just got a call on my work phone. All whispers. High quivery whispers. Said I had to come to the Chandler terrace, claimed they saw me last night with the poker in my hand. A whisper . . . I don't know. It could have been a man. It could have been a woman . . . Wanted me to come and have a little chat . . . I don't know . . . a threat . . . I didn't say a word . . . I'm' – she gave me a funny little smile – 'by myself . . . I won't go anywhere . . . Don, I'm frightened . . . yes, I'll be here.'

I pointed at her work phone. 'Keep that safe. It will show you received a call and the number will be there. But it will probably be a burner phone.'

Acting Chief Harris would accuse Fran of buying a burner phone, calling her own number, keeping the call open long enough to account for a call, then discarding the burner.

'Lock the doors. Get that gun. Don't open the door for anyone but Don.' I disappeared. Don was surely en route to the Chandler house. I joined him in the swift red car.

Don turned off the headlights as the Corvette came around a curve and began the climb to King's Road. He eased to a stop midway up the hill, likely very near where Travis parked his SUV last night.

For a big man, Don moved quietly, melting out of the driver's seat on to the sidewalk, closing the door without a sound. He was almost invisible in a dark sweater and slacks. He reached the path into the woods in two strides. He stopped, listened. With a pocket flashlight cupped in his left hand, he moved silently along the path. The night was still with no wind. An owl whooed in the distance. He used the light sparingly, turned it off at the first glimmer of the lights on the terrace staircase. A step, a pause, another step.

At the edge of the woods, he looked toward the stairs, dark except for the small spots of radiance afforded by the light poles. The owl whooed again. Slowly Don slipped to the foot of the steps, looked up. A faint wash of light was visible from the terrace. No one stood by the railing. Don ran lightly up the stairs. The owl's cry was nearer.

He reached the top of the stairs. The terrace was dark except for a slice of light from the door at the west side of the terrace, the door with the wiped knobs, the red door. That door was ajar, just enough for some light to spill outside.

A woman screamed, a piercing ragged desperate scream. Again. And again.

Don ran toward the open door, yanked it wide, plunged into the hall.

Doors opened. Margaret Foster stood in the doorway of her office. She cried, 'What's wrong?' A barefoot Stuart in baggy sweats peered down the hall. He looked as if he might have been yanked from a nap, his hair mussed, his expression befuddled. Jason Pace squeezed one hand as if still moving a pinball flipper. 'What the hell's going on?'

Elise Douglas clung to the doorjamb of the pool room. 'Help me. Someone help me.' She jerked around, flung herself back toward the pool.

Don ran past her, gave a quick look in the deep end, executed a racing dive, stroked fast to the middle of the pool, arched down.

I gazed down into the water. Don was near the bottom, reaching out to a motionless body. Voices and steps sounded loud and frantic. Margaret rushed to Elise. 'What's wrong?' Stuart Chandler was right behind her. Jason Pace hung back near the doorway, watched.

Elise pointed at the deep end of the pool. 'He's down there.' Her voice shook, her face twisted in despair.

The surface rippled and Don appeared, Dwight Douglas in a rescue hold. Dwight's battered head lolled to one side, a broken neck no longer able to support its weight. As his head rolled, blood seeped from the crushed portion of his skull.

Elise screamed. 'His head. He's hurt. Dwight's hurt.'

Outside sirens wailed.

Don reached the edge of the pool with his burden, gestured to Stuart and Jason. Stuart hurried to the edge. Jason, his face pale, came slowly. As Don supported the dead man, Stuart and Jason each grasped an arm, tugged as Don heaved. The body came up and over the side.

Stuart was on his knees by the dead man, then he pushed up, walked to his sister, wrapped his arms around her rigid body. A few feet away, Margaret looked helpless and frightened. Near the diving board, Jason held to the ladder, bent over, violently retched. Crystal rushed in from the hall. 'I heard sirens. I couldn't find anybody.' She stopped, pressed a hand to her lips. 'Oh my God.' She stumbled to a deckchair, sank down, buried her face in her hands, shuddered.

Judy Weitz and two uniformed officers walked into the room. Judy was weekend casual in a pink sweater, black slacks, and pink tennis shoes. One officer was tall, thin and gray, the other a petite strawberry blonde. A man in a wet suit and several firemen followed. Judy took a quick glance, saw Don and the body, the distraught viewers. She spoke quietly to the firemen and water rescuer and they turned and left. Her gaze took everything in, the body on the pool rim, Don in sopping clothes, the onlookers. She walked up to Don, looked at him in inquiry.

'I got a tip something was up out on the terrace. I came over to check it out. The door was open to the terrace. Then,' he gestured at Elise, 'she screamed. I got here fast. But time wouldn't have helped him. What brought you?'

'Nine-one-one operator buzzed me when they got the emergency call, drowning man in pool. Smart of her to think homicide should check it out since the same address had a dead body last night.'

'Reported as an accident?'

'Right. Message garbled. Man in pool. Come quick to back terrace. We did. Two patrol cars, ambulance, fire truck.'

Don looked around the room. 'Where's Howie?'

Judy's tone was bland. 'Gone to some kind of literary festival. Gets back in town tonight.'

'So you're in charge?'

'Right. And things are getting interesting. You haven't been to the station today so you may not know. Howie doesn't know yet either. Somebody put a note on his desk claiming the murderer entered the house through the red door on the west side of the terrace.' She gestured. 'Note claims there's a witness.'

Don grinned. 'Howie will probably accuse me of writing the note but I wasn't there today.'

'Yeah. Like I said, it's getting interesting. Anyway, the ME is on the way. Techs are coming. Just in case.'

Don gave her a grin. 'Howie will probably dock your pay.'

Her shrug was indifferent. 'Protocol. I'll remind him.'

'I want to be a fly on the wall.'

A brief smile. 'These things happen. Speaking of, you're soaked. You want to go home, get some dry clothes?'

Don gave his shirt sleeve a squeeze. 'I've got a gym bag in my trunk. Take me five minutes.' He strode toward the door.

Judy turned to the silent gathering.

Elise Douglas, head bent, hands tightly clasped, remained in her brother's protective embrace. Crystal Pace huddled in a webbed chair, a beach towel held against her lips. Her face no longer had the glow of healthy exercise, was paper white. Jason still clung to the high dive ladder, his face stark. Margaret Foster didn't look competent and collected. She held tight to the string of pearls that gleamed against a navy sweater, carefully avoided looking at the body huddled on the cement.

Judy approached Elise.

Stuart gave his sister's shoulders a squeeze.

Judy spoke quietly, 'Ma'am, I suggest you go upstairs for now. By law the deceased cannot be moved until the medical examiner has made his investigation. When a death occurs without an attending physician, the police are required to file a report. We' – a nod at the watching group – 'must interview witnesses. We will proceed as quickly as possible.'

Margaret stepped forward. 'I can go with Elise.' Was she

prompted by compassion or a desire to be removed from a grisly scene? Blood still seeped from Dwight's broken head.

Judy nodded approval. 'Thank you.'

Stuart gave his sister's shoulder a final pat as Margaret took Elise's arm. 'Come with me, Elise. I'll help you.'

Elise hung back for a moment, stared at Dwight's body. 'Dwight.' Her deep voice was as forlorn as a loon's cry as night falls.

Margaret gave a gentle tug. Elise sagged against her. Elise looked old and lost, walked in a stoop, Margaret's hand gripping one arm.

No one spoke as the two women slowly crossed to the door and out into the hall. As the sound of their steps receded, everyone stared at Judy Weitz – Stuart fidgeting near the enclosure for the pool toys, Crystal hunched in her chair, the beach towel pressed against her lips, Jason clinging to the steel ladder for support.

Judy turned away and walked to the pool edge, looked down at Dwight's body.

Don was already garbed in warmup pants and a sweatshirt. He slammed the trunk shut, tapped the cell phone in his free hand. 'Another death here. Stay locked in . . . Don't answer unless you know the caller . . . Keep your doors locked . . . It will be late . . . Right.' He clicked off, tucked the phone in a pocket, moved fast. He reached the terrace, nodded to the officer at the open door, entered the pool room, joined Judy beside the body.

Footsteps sounded and three techs, two middle-aged men, one lean, one plump, the third with purple hair and dangly earrings, walked in with their equipment. Judy gave them a come-here wave as she spoke to Don. 'The secretary is taking the widow upstairs. I'll go up as soon as I get the techs started.'

Don looked at the body. Dwight's head quirked to one side. A gaping wound disfigured the right side of his skull. There were no other signs of trauma. Dwight lay on his back, long arms outspread, legs apart. A big man, he looked oddly small lying on the concrete.

I understood now what happened. Dwight didn't live long

enough to take his eight fifteen selfie. He came to the pool at his regular time, a quarter to eight, walked into the big, quiet high-ceilinged room with the pool and diving board, deckchairs and a wet bar. A large container with netted sides held pool playthings, balls, boogie boards, life rings, plastic floats. Now the room seemed crowded, Judy and Don, the crime techs, the silent onlookers, and the body. Crime techs in their usual fashion worked from the perimeter toward the center, in this case from the edges of the room toward the pool, sketching, photographing, filming, measuring.

Swift steps sounded. I recognized the ME, trim, fast-moving Jacob Brandt, brown hair shaggy and a little long. He was in weekend gray sweats, a red bandana around his head instead of a sweatband. His flushed face suggested the summons reached him when he was out for a night run. He carried a black leather bag. He moved toward Judy and Don, gave them a brief wave, turned to look down at the body. 'Took a whack.' He lifted his head, checked out the diving platform. His eyes moved from the board back to the body, likely estimating whether a dive went wrong, very wrong, what surface had been struck to result in trauma.

I don't know anything about diving. I've seen people somersault, swan dive, spring high off a board. Dwight Douglas looked tough and athletic, likely enjoyed fancy dives.

I looked around the pool area. The catch-all for playthings was behind the chair where Crystal sat, the beach towel still pressed to her mouth.

The other side of the pool, the far side from where the body lay and Judy and Don stood, was equipped for emergencies. Two rescue poles were lodged on metal supports, one above the other, perhaps a foot apart, and easily within reach. The lower pole was about five feet from the cement floor.

The last time I was here, my gaze swept over those poles. And yes, the top pole then lay straight and true on its support. The top pole now was perhaps an inch or so askew.

Jacob Brandt returned the stethoscope to his black bag, snapped it shut, popped to his feet with the grace of an athletic young man. He looked again from the body to the diving board as he walked toward the detectives. 'Have to do the PM to be sure but I think a broken neck killed him. Major head trauma. If it was a back alley, I'd say a blackjack got him. I suppose he could have slipped from the board.' He gestured at the diving board with his thumb. 'Maybe he was doing a double twist and threw himself on to the edge of the pool. You can check surfaces for blood, brain tissue. Maybe he had a heart attack.' A glance at the body. 'Looks healthy enough but I'll find out. Cardiac arrest could cause a violent lurch off the high dive into the side of the pool. Or—'

Crack.

The sudden unexpected sound brought instant silence. Every head jerked to look across the pool.

One end of the upper rescue pole now rested on the concrete. I easily dislodged it with a tap.

Judy and Don moved swiftly, swung around the end of the pool, passing the ladder to the high dive. They stopped a scant foot from the long thin pole, looked down, then raised their eyes to study the empty bracket.

Don's gaze moved to the pole still aloft, then again at the top pole with one end against its bracket, the other end on the concrete. 'Maybe somebody was in a hurry, perched the pole but didn't get it snug in both brackets.'

At shortly after a quarter to eight, Dwight entered the pool room. His terrycloth robe lay on a chair perhaps six feet from the netted container for playthings.

I pictured him as he walked toward the end of the pool, turning, going up the ladder to the high dive. He would have had no reason to look toward the netted enclosure where someone waited with the rescue pole clutched in both hands. Dwight climbed the steps with no sense of unease. On the board perhaps he went to the end, bounced a few times, finally landed hard and flew into the air and somersaulted down into the deep end. The watcher moved fast and was ready with the pole raised. The instant Dwight reached the surface, the pole slammed down on his head. A tense moment of waiting. But Dwight would not come up from the bottom of the pool. The pole then was dipped in the water, a cloth used to polish away fingerprints. Possibly the murderer wore gloves. I felt certain the pole would yield no trace of fingerprints. In a hurry, the murderer ran around the end of the pool to return the pole to its brackets and then the swift escape from the pool room. Opening the hall door, listening, slipping out unseen.

It was as if Judy knew my thoughts. She pointed at the still water below the diving board. 'Let's say he does a dive, comes up. Somebody standing at the edge of the pool with the pole cracks his head open, snaps his neck.'

Don nodded. 'A hell of a blow.'

'Yeah.' Judy's blue eyes, cool now, measured the silent group watching them. 'Think it's time we got some statements. I'll do the widow and the secretary. You see to the rest of them.'

'My pleasure.' A twisted smile. 'I should mention Howie intends to formally censure me. I took—'

Judy interrupted. 'I heard all about it. Big Bad Don and Murderous Fran had a fun day. We can sort all of that out later with Howie. It's not a problem for me, Detective Smith.' Judy gestured at a tech near the diving board. The girl with purple hair hustled over.

Judy pointed at the dangling rescue pole. 'Handle that baby with care, Ann. I suspect it's been in the water but look for blood under ultraviolet. It could be the weapon.'

Ann nodded energetically, purple hair quivering. 'I'll get some pix then wrap her up, take her to the lab.'

Judy looked across the pool where Stuart, Crystal and Jason waited. 'I'll go up and talk to the widow.'

Don caught the attention of the young officer in the doorway. 'I'll detail Russell to escort the family members to a comfortable spot to wait.' He looked at Stuart. 'I'll start with bro. He isn't soused tonight. Could easily slam a man over the head.'

Judy's gaze swept the trio on the other side of the pool. 'Let's play it like an accident for now. See what we can get. Maybe at the end a quick question about the rescue pole.'

I liked her tone. As we say in Oklahoma, she was on her horse and ready to ride.

ELEVEN

'He swam every evening.' Elise's voice quivered. She looked small and very alone on a big-cushioned sofa. The crimson robe and plaid squares of the upholstery made an odd combination. Her face was utterly colorless except for patches of blush.

Judy Weitz slipped a small black recorder from a pocket, turned it on, spoke quietly, 'Detective Weitz. Interview with Mrs Elise Douglas.' She added the date and time, put the recorder on a coffee table. 'Tell me about tonight.'

The large black bird in the cage near the bedroom door moved on his perch and squawked.

Tears brimmed, streaked her cheeks. 'He was having so much fun after that other detective made such a huge deal of where everyone was at eight fifteen last night.'

'Other detective?' Judy's tone called for a reply.

The bird cocked his head, rustled his wings.

'A redhead. Very plain suit. Detective Loy. She has the figure for good clothes. Maybe in her late twenties.'

The bird cawed.

'Detective Loy.' Judy repeated the name. 'She was here earlier today?'

Elise sagged against the back of the sofa. 'This afternoon. She wanted to know where everyone was at eight fifteen last night. We asked her what difference did it make. She said something about information received. I don't know. Maybe she wanted to know if any of us saw that woman.'

'Woman?' Judy looked confused.

Margaret said quickly, 'The antique dealer. The one pictured in the security footage.'

Judy well knew the time Fran Loring was photographed. Eight twenty-two. 'Eight fifteen,' she repeated thoughtfully.

Margaret was impatient. 'I don't think any of this matters now. Dwight was having fun. At dinner he persuaded everyone to go to the spot where they were last night and take a selfie, something silly.'

Judy wasn't deflected. 'Did Detective Loy explain why the time mattered?'

The bird pecked on a bar, cawed.

Elise spoke dully. 'Not really. She only said the question arose because of information received. I don't know what that means. Anyway, Dwight made a game out of it at dinner and said we all had to take selfies of exactly where we were at eight fifteen. He always went down to swim about a quarter to eight and was coming away from the pool at eight fifteen. I guess,' her voice wobbled, 'he didn't get to take his selfie.' A struggle for breath. 'I took mine. I started to read and then I realized he was late coming up. He always swam for half an hour. I called and he didn't answer. I called and—'

Judy interrupted quietly, 'He would have his phone with him at the pool?'

Elise was impatient. 'Are you listening? I told you. He said we all had to take pictures where we were at eight fifteen last night and that's where he was. Of course he had his phone with him. But I called and there was no answer. So I went down.' A shudder. 'And he was lying on the bottom of the pool.' She pressed her hands against her face.

The bird looked down at her, cawed.

Margaret patted her shoulder. 'Elise, let me get you a Valium.' She looked at Judy. 'Elise needs to rest.'

Judy rose. 'I will send Mrs Pace up to relieve you. Please come downstairs then so we can speak with you.'

As Judy walked swiftly to the stairs, she spoke into her cell. 'Have we got a new hire, a redheaded detective named Loy? . . . Right. Thanks.' Her face crinkled in a puzzled frown.

Judy Weitz gestured to the purple-haired tech. 'Have you found a cell phone?'

'Nope.'

Judy glanced at the terrycloth robe on the beach chair. 'Check that out.'

I supposed Judy wanted to confirm Elise's statement that

she called several times. Perhaps she hoped Dwight took his selfie when he arrived rather than planning to take it as he departed.

The tech took pix from each side, used an attached stylus to sketch on her iPad. She put aside the camera and iPad, pulled on plastic gloves, carefully lifted the robe. After checking to make sure nothing had fallen free, she eased open one side pocket, probed with a stiff piece of plastic, repeated the search of the other pocket. 'No cell phone.'

Judy looked at the large container of pool toys, pointed. 'Give it a look. Search every inch of this place. I want that cell phone.'

I wondered with a chill if Judy hoped to catch Elise in a lie. I never doubted Elise's grief. But what would Elise do if she killed Sylvia and Dwight was toying with her?

In the masculine room with the overstuffed leather furniture and dart target, Don placed the recorder on a coffee table, turned it on.

Stuart Chandler watched with interest. His eyes were clear, his round face firm. No slack muscles tonight. 'How come sometimes you record and sometimes you don't.'

Don was pleasant. 'It's customary when interviewing witnesses.'

Stuart nodded. 'But she didn't tape me this afternoon.'

'Who didn't tape you?'

'The redheaded detective.' His face creased. 'A pretty tough lady.'

I was complimented. Then I eschewed the thought. I wasn't ready to sniff coal smoke.

Don nodded. 'Remember her name?'

Stuart looked embarrassed. 'I'm bad with names. Kind of a funny name. Oh I know. I make up a little sentence to help me. Hers was Not a Boy. So it was something like boy. Not toy. Or Coy. Oh, yeah. Loy. Detective Loy.'

'What did she ask you about?'

Stuart looked uncomfortable. 'A bunch of stuff.' He didn't want to talk about money or Sylvia's life interest. 'She mostly wanted to know where everyone was at eight fifteen last night,

and the funny thing is it turns out four of us were down here.'
He gestured toward the hall. 'Dwight at the pool. Margaret in
her office. Me here. Jason in the pinball room. Only Elise and
Crystal were upstairs. Anyway, at dinner Dwight thought it
would be a hoot if we all took a selfie where we were and
we'd have a contest. Dwight was bored. He's used to lots of
action, ran a big lumber yard. Hanging around here waiting
for my dad to die wasn't his idea of fun. God, poor Elise.'
Stuart's eyes were brooding. 'Dwight's all she had. That and
her shop. I mean, maybe my life's all screwed up but I've got
two kids and . . . Anyway, that's why we were all where we
were tonight.'

Don kept on track. 'You were here at eight fifteen. And
afterward?'

Stuart took a swipe at his rumpled hair. 'I stretched out on
the sofa. I fell asleep. And then I heard screams.'

Crystal's eyes were glazed with shock. 'I've been waiting.
They told me, that policeman, to stay here and you'd come.
I don't know what anyone can tell you. Dwight's head.' Crystal
clasped her hands together and a huge diamond in her wedding
ring glittered in the lamplight.

Judy Weitz put the recorder on an end table, turned it on,
repeated the preface to an interview. 'Did you know Dwight
went to the pool every evening?'

'Everyone knew.' Her tone was waspish. 'He dared Jason
to do a double somersault. Jason does machines. Jason is in
great shape.'

Clearly Jason didn't measure up as far as his brother-in-law
was concerned.

'Did you see Dwight in the pool?'

'Oh.' A stricken breath. 'So awful.'

'Before the accident?'

Crystal swallowed jerkily. 'Was it an accident? I'm scared.
Sylvia last night. Dwight tonight. Oh, I don't think it was an
accident.'

Don waited in the hallway near the door to Margaret's office.

Judy came quickly down the hall, faced him. 'Anything?'

'Same old, same old. All the little mice in their holes. Nobody heard or saw anything.'

'Yeah.' She sounded abstracted. 'I checked the station. Nobody sneaked in a new hire without telling me. There is no Detective Loy. What the hell do you suppose?'

Don's shoulders lifted and fell. 'Only thing that occurs to me is maybe Howie asked OSBI for an agent. Why he would, though, I don't know.'

'Maybe the department doesn't have to pay the Oklahoma State Bureau of Investigation anything for assistance. Howie saving a buck. I guess not ours to reason why. We're just working stiffs.' Judy jerked a head toward Margaret's door. 'Let's see if she knows anything.' She knocked, opened the door.

Margaret sat behind her desk, looked like a woman staring into a cauldron of snakes. 'Come in.' She gestured at chairs. 'This is unbelievable.'

Judy pulled a chair a little closer to Margaret's desk, placed the recorder there, clicked it on. She spoke her piece as Don settled on the other straight chair.

Margaret's expression was somber. 'Have you looked at the selfie on Dwight's phone?'

Judy shook her head. 'We're looking for the phone. Let me check.' She pulled out her cell, tapped. 'Any sign of the victim's cell phone? . . . See if the widow's phone can track it. Let me know.'

Margaret picked up a pencil, rolled it in her fingers. She looked puzzled. 'The selfies were Dwight's idea. I'm surprised you haven't found the phone.' Several taps with the pencil.

I wondered if the taps were meant as a rebuke to police inefficiency.

Judy said nothing.

Margaret's voice was high. 'I'm frightened.'

Don spoke quietly. 'What frightens you, Mrs Foster?'

The older woman's lips trembled. 'What doesn't frighten me. Someone came into the library from the terrace last night and killed Sylvia. And tonight Elise screamed and I ran out into the hall and the door was open to the terrace and Dwight was on the bottom of the pool. Something's terribly wrong.'

Don was gentle. 'Take a deep breath, Mrs Foster. Another.'
He gave her an encouraging smile. 'You can help us. You're
perceptive, alert. I expect your subconscious has picked up
a sense of danger. When did you first begin to feel
frightened?'

Margaret breathed deeply, quietly, looked chagrined. 'I'm
sorry. I don't know what's the matter with me.'

Judy was calm. 'Detective Smith's right, you know. You
are someone who is attuned to the people around you. You've
spent your life working for this family. Something has disturbed
you. Is it connected to Dwight's plan for everyone to take a
selfie?'

'I don't think so.' She didn't sound certain. 'Oh maybe.'
The pencil tapped.

Judy clicked off the recorder. 'If you remember anything
out of the ordinary, a look, a sound—' Judy's cell rang.
She looked, tapped, listened. 'Order a search tomorrow
morning.' She clicked off. 'Mr Chandler's cell phone is
somewhere in the woods behind the house. We'll find it
tomorrow.'

Margaret's face squeezed in thought. Several taps of the pencil.
'I don't understand how his cell phone can be in the woods.' A
pause. 'Oh, the terrace door was open.' She spoke slowly as if
picturing a flight. 'Someone took his phone and threw it into the
woods. How odd.' She sounded bewildered.

I struggled to understand as well. Everyone knows cell
phones can be located. There could be no advantage to tossing
Dwight's phone into the woods where it would surely be found.
I felt a deep sense of foreboding. The cell phone would not
reveal a selfie. But the murderer, the quick thinking, active
murderer, was executing a plan. Dwight dead. His phone
thrown. Why?

Judy picked up as if there had been no interruption. 'If you
feel uneasy, have any sense of danger, call us.' Judy pulled a
card from her pocket, placed it on the desk. 'Any time of the
day or night.'

At the door, Don turned and said quietly, 'It might be wise
for the residents to keep their doors locked.'

*   *   *

In the pool room, a tech checked the pix on his laptop.

Judy and Don walked up to him.

The tech paused. 'About to close up. They took the body away half an hour ago.'

'Any surprises?'

The tech shook his head.

Judy nodded. 'Shut it down.' Judy looked at Don. 'Meet me at the station?'

'In half an hour.'

Judy gave him a steady gaze, shrugged. 'Whatever.'

I gave a last look at the pool, the water utterly still. The only surprise tonight occurred when Dwight Chandler's head broke the surface and death descended. He'd arranged for everyone to take a selfie at eight fifteen to show their location on Friday night. Dwight was the only one who wasn't able to complete the plan. So why did the murderer remove his cell phone from the pool and throw it into the woods. Where it would be found.

Fran stared at the grandfather clock. A quarter to midnight. She stood up, paced back and forth. Her face was pale, tight with fear. The doorbell rang. She turned, ran, grabbed the knob, stopped, pulled open the peephole, checked. She opened the door, flung it wide. In an instant she was wrapped in Don's arms. 'I am so scared.'

He stepped back a little, put his hand under her chin. 'I know. I'm scared too. I don't know if I should be here.'

She stared at him for a frozen instant, then her face crumpled and she pulled away.

'Oh hell.' He reached out, grabbed her, held her tight. 'I'm here for you. Now. Always. Don't ever look like that, Fran. I meant I might have been smarter not to come, let you be contacted tomorrow and not know anything about what happened. I don't know what's smarter for you.'

Her voice was muffled against his shoulder. 'That awful call. And someone else dead. If I'd gone there . . . someone is trying to get me blamed.'

'Yeah.' His voice was grim. 'Come on. Let's sit down.'

They settled on the rosewood settee. Don gripped her hands in his. 'I've got to go to the station when I leave here. I have to explain why I showed up just in time to hear Elise Douglas scream. Whoever called you hoped you'd be there when all hell broke loose. If you had . . .' He took a deep breath. 'It's bad, Fran. A body on the bottom of the pool. Cracked head. Broken neck. Ninety per cent sure he was murdered. Now, I want you to get a little something to eat. Then I think we should go to the station together. You come in voluntarily. A good citizen.'

The break room held three small tables with four chairs each. Dingy pale green walls were more reminiscent of pond scum than a peaceful glen. Three Wanted posters decorated one wall, a detailed street map of Adelaide on another. But the break room wasn't a grey-walled interrogation room with intense light pointed at a single chair.

A round clock on the wall, white face, black arms, reminded me of classroom days. Ten minutes after midnight.

Judy Weitz stood by a coffee maker. 'We have regular. Decaf. Or tea. Or soda.' Despite the late hour and her long day, Judy's pleasant face was composed, her blue eyes alert.

'Coffee. Regular.' Don looked at Fran.

'Decaf, please.' Her golden ringlets were neatly brushed. Her sensitive face, bare of makeup, looked frightened but determined.

Don helped serve. Judy took a seat opposite Fran, Don to her right. Judy placed the recorder on the table, looked inquiringly at Fran, then Don.

'Mrs Loring is here to assist the police in their inquiry.' He reached out a long arm, flicked on the recorder.

Judy briskly recited date, time, matter under investigation, contributing parties. She looked at Fran. 'You believe you have relevant information?'

'I do. I was at home alone this evening when my work cell phone rang.' She slipped the phone from a pocket, tapped Recent Calls. 'The call came at eight thirty-three. I answered, said, "Mitchell Antiques. How may I help you?"' Fran's lips quivered. 'The call was dreadful. A whisper and a threat,

"Better help yourself, Fran Loring. I saw you last night" – a tight breath – "with the poker in your hand. Didn't know I was there, did you? Let's get together, have a little talk. Be at the railing by the terrace steps ASAP."'

Don reached over, gripped her hand.

Fran shot him a grateful glance, but her eyes were dark with fear.

'And?' Judy prompted.

'I just held the phone for a minute, stared at it. I was terrified. That whisper. And none of it was true. None of it. Sylvia was dead when I went inside. I ran right out. I never saw anyone, heard anyone. I looked at the phone and knew I was in danger. Someone – oh it must have been the person who killed Sylvia – called me, wanted me to come there. I was sure something awful had happened. I called Don. He said to stay home and lock the doors. I did. And I waited and waited.' She looked at Judy, turned to Don. 'And now someone else is dead.'

Judy was brisk. 'Presumably everyone went to the spot they'd occupied at eight fifteen the night before.'

Don recited their names, where they claimed to be. Elise and Crystal in their separate suites upstairs. Downstairs a row of rooms, Jason Pace playing pinball, Stuart Chandler comfortable on a leather sofa, Margaret Foster in her office, Dwight Douglas in the swimming pool.

Don continued, 'Douglas went down to the pool at a quarter to eight. He always swam for half an hour. When he didn't come back, his wife called his cell. No answer. She tried several times. No answer. She went down to the pool. I'd just reached the terrace when I heard her screams. The west terrace door was open. I ran inside. He was on the bottom of the pool. I brought him up. Bashed head, broken neck.'

'Why call me?' Fran demanded. 'I don't know those people and how could anyone there know me?'

Judy took a sip. 'The residents of the house were shown the security footage of you on the terrace last night. Likely someone there recognized you.'

Don looked disgusted. 'Oh swell, let's show the suspects – not that Howie will admit they are suspects – the photo of a trespasser, and hey someone said, oh that's Fran Loring, she has that antique shop.' He turned to Fran. 'The call came on your business cell.'

Fran looked relieved. 'Of course that's what happened. That's how someone knew who I was. That makes sense. The murderer saw the footage and called me tonight to try and get me to come there. Even if I hadn't picked up, I'll bet that whispery message would be left.'

Judy held out her hand. 'May I see your work cell?'

Fran opened her purse, found the phone, handed it to Judy.

Judy looked. 'Call came at eight thirty-three. Let me run a check on the number.' She returned Fran's phone, picked up her own. In a moment, she lifted her head, looked from Fran to Don. 'Mobile number for Dwight Douglas.'

Fran looked puzzled.

Don's face hardened. 'Oh, Christ.'

TWELVE

Fran put a hand on the passenger door handle. 'You don't need to see me—'

Don turned off the ignition. 'Don't be silly.'

She reached out, touched his arm. 'I'm in a mess. It isn't your mess. Today was perfect until I got that call. I shouldn't have called you. God, I don't want to ruin your career. Go home. Forget you ever saw me.'

He was out of the car and walking to the other side.

I grabbed her arm, ignored her startled jerk, whispered: 'Tell him Detective Loy came to see you this afternoon and told you that you were in the clear because the murderer re-entered the house at eight fifteen and you were taped on the security footage at eight twenty-two.'

The car door opened. Don stood, big, strong, and determined. He held out his hand.

Fran slipped out on to the drive, closed the door. 'Don, you have to forget—'

He pulled her into a tight embrace, spoke with his face against her hair. 'I won't forget. I'll never forget. You—'

Some moments are not meant for me.

After the early service Sunday morning at St Mildred's, I strolled to the cemetery adjacent to the church. Though the morning was cold, the sun was shining. I added a warm muffler to a navy wool coat and walked briskly. The Pritchard Mausoleum gleamed in the early morning sun. All Adeladians know where to go for a spot of luck. I stepped inside and walked to the head of Hannah's tomb and gently stroked the whiskers of a sleek marble Abyssinian cat. Maurice's resting place was overseen by an elegant marble greyhound. I patted the muscular dog's side. I remembered the Pritchards well. They were movers and shakers when I was a young woman in Adelaide. I remembered a joyful Christmas feast at their grand home and the cat streaking from the kitchen with a turkey leg firmly gripped in her small mouth and the large dog romping along behind her and I swear he was laughing. Now they were marble. Once they were warm and living and beloved.

As I turned to go, I gave the dog and cat a decided nod. 'Be my four-leaf clover, sweeties.' I – and Fran – needed all the luck we could gather.

An unshaven, tousle-haired Don looked very masculine and appealing at Fran's breakfast table. He still wore the warmups. Fran was dressed in a gold turtleneck and brown slacks, but she still wore house shoes.

Don gave a contented sigh and rested his fork on the plate. 'Lady, that's the best frittata I've ever eaten.'

She smiled. 'Thank you.' She too put down her fork, but there was a considerable heap of bell-pepper-studded eggs on her plate. 'You've never asked me about Friday night. Saturday was a happy day. A free day. Maybe one of my last free days.' Her voice was steady with an effort. 'And last night I told you to go home, that I didn't want to ruin your career—'

He interrupted. 'Like I said then, protecting an innocent woman is what a good cop does. That's what I'm doing. And will do.'

'You never asked me why I was on that damn terrace.' She took a deep breath. 'Friday night I went to my brother's house for dinner . . .'

The central area with desks for detectives – I counted nine desks – was unoccupied. Judy Weitz's desk drawers were locked, the computer screen blank. No doubt Judy duly changed passwords every week and never shared a one.

Howie Harris's temporary office was unoccupied. As before, his computer was on and accessible. At shortly after one a.m., Judy e-mailed her report on the death of Dwight Douglas. I skimmed until I reached the last few paragraphs. The facts were damning for Fran: she received a call from Dwight Douglas's cell phone at eight thirty-three p.m. Don arrived on the terrace in response to Fran's call to him. The call to nine-one-one originated on Dwight's cell phone at eight thirty-five. A double whammy.

Dwight's cell phone. I imagined what it might show if he had lived to leave the pool at eight fifteen. The photo would feature his tough face staring up the hallway by the pool. What did he see? He saw a murderer hurrying to sanctuary, either to Margaret's office or Stuart's leather retreat or Jason's pinball haven or upstairs to Elise's suite or Crystal's.

That knowledge prompted Dwight's 'selfie game'. He wanted the murderer to know he held freedom in the balance. Would he inform the police? Likely not. He was, in his own mordant way, exerting power. *I know.* In his arrogance, he felt he was in charge. But the murderer made certain Dwight would never take his selfie. His repeated emphasis on eight fifteen twisted the knife.

Dwight was likely in high good humor when he entered the pool room. I pictured him slapping across the concrete to a deckchair, pulling off his robe with the cell phone in a pocket. A man who focused on the moment, he swung around and headed for the high dive. He wouldn't bother to look around the enclosure for playthings. He was big, bold Dwight ready to flex muscles, and take pride in his prowess. He went swiftly up the ladder. Perhaps he stood for a moment, gazing down at the water, loosening up a bit, rocking back and forth on his heels. Then to the end of the board, a jump and the thrill of being airborne, curling down down down into the water, then curving up to regain the surface.

Incredible pain.

I pictured the murderer gripping the pole, likely breathing fast, waiting.

Bubbles on the surface and then the water was still.

The murderer, likely wearing gloves this night, poked the bloody end of the pole into the water, moved the pole back and forth, fast, faster. Perhaps the pole was pulled up, studied, plunged again into the pool for a violent swish. Satisfied, the murderer ran around the end of the pool to the empty brackets, pushed the pole in place, but didn't lodge the pole securely. The murderer ran back around the end of the pool to the terrycloth robe lying on the chair, picked it up, found Dwight's cell phone. The murderer dashed to the hall door, eased it open. No one in sight. Quickly the murderer ran to the terrace door, pulled it open to suggest an outside intruder. Then the murderer escaped to a safe place to call Fran, make the whispered threat, call nine-one-one.

The calls from Dwight Douglas's cell phone enmeshed Fran in an ever-tightening net. Detective M. Loy's job wasn't done. But she would be revealed as an imposter, a pretender soon. Unless . . .

I looked at Sam's face and felt a burst of joy. I didn't need to be told the good news. His mother was recovering. This wasn't her time to enter the gate to larger life.

Sam stood in the middle of the small kitchen holding perhaps a dozen pansies in one big hand. He lifted them up to show Claire. 'Do you think you can find me a little vase? Mom loves pansies.'

Claire was at the oven door. 'Hold on a minute.' She opened the oven, used two big hot pads to remove one cake pan, carry it to the counter. She returned for the other.

I sniffed. Mmm.

'Smells great.' Sam sounded eager and hungry.

'Burnt sugar cake.' Claire was rummaging beneath the sink. She came up with a narrow-necked small vase. 'This will do.' She put the vase under the cold faucet, filled it three-quarters full.

'Burnt sugar.' Sam sounded happy. 'Mom's favorite.' He was at the kitchen door, pushing through. In the hall, I tapped him on the shoulder. 'Sam.' A soft voice.

He swung in the direction of the touch.

'Sam, it's Officer Loy. Actually this time Detective—'

He didn't look a bit surprised. His smile was broad and welcoming. 'I thought you'd get in touch. Don called this morning.'

I had a moment of panic.

'I told him not to worry. Sure, the redheaded detective had to be from OSBI. I'm going to give Howie a ring, explain this happens in some cases, that I'd heard from Higher Powers so not to worry, just be polite and give her free rein. I'll tell him he's doing a great job and that – the best part of Detective Loy – she always gives the credit to the man in charge.'

'Higher Powers,' I whispered. 'I like that. Thank you, Sam.'

The hearse in the circular drive at the Chandler house startled me. Then I understood. The gates of larger life had been opened to Arthur Chandler.

Stuart and Margaret were in the great entrance hall. Margaret held the door wide. The gurney was eased down the steps, wheeled outside, Arthur's final departure.

Margaret gently closed the door, leaned her forehead against the wood. Stuart slipped an arm around her shoulders. 'You helped Dad build a great company. And then you smoothed the path for Sylvia. She appreciated you.'

Margaret stood straight. Her eyes glistened with tears. 'I loved working with your father. He was intuitive about where to drill. Oh yes, he had the maps and knew the formations but somehow he was like a dowsing rod. When he said, "Drill," we found oil. It was exciting. It was like climbing a mountain. Sheer cliffs and lots of crevasses,' pink touched her cheeks, 'but we always got there.'

'Yes. You did. And now . . .' There was uncertainty in his voice.

Margaret gripped his arm. 'Come home, Stuart. You and Melissa and Jimmy and Phoebe. You can take Chandler Exploration even higher.'

His rounded face looked forlorn. 'Dad never thought—'

She put her fingers gently against his lips. 'Arthur was good at finding oil. He was big and strong and athletic and reckless. He didn't understand who you were and he saw your kindness as a weakness. He didn't think you were tough. And maybe you aren't tough. But I'm tough. I remember when you were first out of school. You had his touch. The fields you wanted us to try later on proved to be big wells. Big wells. You may not be like Arthur in many ways but you have that instinct.'

He looked wistful. 'I think I could make a go of it. But Sylvia was pretty far along with the sale, wasn't she?'

Margaret shook her head emphatically. 'You know Sylvia. She always thought she could get a better deal. She'd decided to let them dangle for awhile, let the Woodford shale do even better. She said maybe in a year or so. Not now.'

Stuart rubbed the side of his face. 'Be damn fun, wouldn't it?' He gave her a quick hug. 'Maybe. We'll see what happens. Right now I've got to deal with' – he spread his hand – 'all of this. There's the service for Sylvia Thursday, I've got to help Elise. She wants to take Dwight home, have a memorial for him there. And Crystal.' His smile was sweet. 'I'll take care of Crystal and Jason. Funny thing is, I think their son is a lot like Dad. I can see him in the company someday.'

'But what about your Jimmy?'

Stuart grinned. 'Jimmy will end up in Hollywood. He's got it all planned. UCLA or bust. And that's fine with me. Who would think Melissa and I would have a kid who can act? Life is strange, Margaret. Anyway, I'll get busy. Will you start planning the right memorial service for Dad? I want to have a big one.'

'Oh yes.' Margaret spoke with vigor, her eyes alight. 'I'll get to work right now.'

Elise was dressed in black. No jewelry. No makeup. Sleek black hair framed a face whiter than a cloud. She sat in a wing chair in the gloomy living room beneath a medieval tapestry with all the warmth of arctic tundra. In her hands she held a framed photograph of Dwight. She was a grieving widow. Yet I remembered her exchange with Dwight when he asked her why she told Detective Loy that she and Dwight were together in her suite at eight fifteen Friday night and her curious expression when he asked, 'Do you need an alibi?' What was their relationship? His face was hard. He looked tough, a man it might be dangerous to cross. Was he taunting her, saying I know you killed Sylvia? At this moment she appeared plunged in grief, battered, devastated. But if she'd coolly managed two murders that would be the role she would play.

Jason twined the cord around the handles of the jump rope. 'Trying to keep in shape. Didn't think it would look right to go for a run.'

Stuart clapped his brother-in-law on the shoulder. 'Go on

out, Jason. Dad never worried about other people's rules. He'd laugh and tell you to run hard.'

Jason shot a quick glance at Crystal. 'OK, hon?'

'You get out for awhile.' As the door closed, Crystal tried to smile. 'You've always been nice to Jason.'

Stuart sat beside her on the small linen-covered sofa. 'Tough time for everybody, Crys. I just wanted to let you know Margaret and I will see to everything. You and Jason can get home for awhile. I don't think we'll have the memorial for a month or so. I want to let everything quiet down about Sylvia and Dwight.'

Crystal looked as if a burden lifted. 'Oh Stuart, thank you. I want to go home.'

He gave her arm a squeeze. 'You and Jason don't need to worry. Margaret and I will see to everything.'

Crystal's eyes were dark with memory. 'I can't get that awful picture out of my mind, Dwight lying by the pool. Oh, I can't make it go away.'

THIRTEEN

I was on the front porch ringing the bell, Detective Loy in her sensible suit, when a patrol car pulled up in the drive. The young blonde officer who'd brought the laptop with the footage of Fran yesterday – oh yes, her name was Bledsoe – stepped out of the car. I gave her a wave.

She looked a little surprised but climbed the steps, blonde ponytail swinging, and stood beside me.

'Officer Bledsoe, good to see you. I'm Detective Loy from OSBI. I'm lending a hand in the investigation.' I looked inquisitive.

Officer Bledsoe said quickly, eager to show the Adelaide police were on their toes, 'I'm organizing a search for the missing cell phone.' She turned and waved at an SUV. 'Here's my team.' The big vehicle disgorged four officers, one dumpy, one pencil thin, one Gene Kelly lithe, and one very likely a former basketball player.

I nodded approvingly. 'I'll inform the family so you can get right to work.'

As the searchers disappeared around the corner of the house, I wondered if they'd been dispatched by Judy Weitz. If Howie Harris was worried about overtime, he wouldn't be happy.

I put my finger on the bell.

Stuart Chandler opened the door, stepped back for me to enter.

I was soft-spoken. 'I saw the hearse. I'm sorry about your father.'

'Thank you.' Stuart held the door open for me.

I stepped inside. 'There are still some questions about last night.'

He looked at me somberly. 'Was my brother-in-law murdered?'

'The evidence suggests so. The autopsy report hasn't been received.'

'Dwight was a champion diver. On a college team. There's no way he could have made that kind of mistake in a dive.' His voice was heavy.

'Why do you think he was killed?'

There was a flicker of shock in his eyes. 'Why?'

I waited. The water splashed softly in the entrance-hall fountain. Otherwise there was not a breath of sound. I watched Stuart think. He'd decided Dwight's death could not be accidental. He hadn't faced the implications.

'Dwight bullied people.' He spoke with regret.

'Is that how you saw his selfie game?'

'Now I do. I only thought he was having a macabre joke for a while. But now . . . He saw someone in the hall that night, didn't he?' Lips pressed together, then as if speaking to himself. 'If he saw someone in the hall . . . If he was coming out of the pool and someone killed Sylvia and came inside from the terrace . . .' A little lurch of breath as if he struggled for air.

I didn't have to list the possibilities. Elise, Crystal, Jason, Margaret. Himself.

He said quickly, 'Last night. With Dwight. The door was open to the terrace.'

I gave him a steady look. 'Of course.'

'Oh damn, damn, damn.' Stuart wheeled away, headed for the stairs. He took the steps two at a time, pounded to the balcony, was out of sight.

Elise remained in the wing chair, Dwight's picture in her hands. She didn't look up as I approached.

I spoke gently. 'Mrs Douglas.'

Dark eyes locked with mine. 'She killed my husband.'

I caught my breath. 'She?'

'That woman, the one on the terrace. They showed us her picture. Why haven't you arrested her? Why did you let her kill my husband?'

I chose my words carefully. 'If you are referring to Mrs Loring, she arrived on the terrace after Mrs Chandler was killed.'

Elise carefully placed the photograph on a side table, pushed up, stood inches from me. 'Did you see her face? And the door was open last night, too.'

'Yes.' I spoke as one might to a survivor of horror. 'You are correct to believe Sylvia's murderer re-entered the house from the terrace. But according to one witness, the murderer had come and gone before Mrs Loring climbed the hill to the terrace. The witness can testify that the murderer re-entered the house through the red door at eight fifteen. Mrs Loring was captured on the security camera at eight twenty-two.'

She gripped my arm, her long nails sharp against my skin. 'I don't believe that witness. I saw her face on the security tape.'

Hatred for Fran made her mask-like face even harder. 'She killed Dwight.' A rasp.

Elise dismissed any possibility the murderer might live in the house. Was she protecting herself? Or someone close to her?

As Mama always told us kids, 'Beating your head against a stone wall doesn't hurt the wall.'

'Your husband went down to the pool last night for a purpose.'

Coal-black eyes stared at me.

'Why did Dwight make a game of selfies at eight fifteen?'

She loosed her grip, sank back into the chair. 'I warned him.' She lifted a haunted face. 'You told us that door closed at eight fifteen. You told everyone. I asked Dwight. I said were you looking out in the hall then? Maybe he saw that antique woman. Maybe there was something she wanted to get in the house. I asked him and he laughed. But I know that laugh. His gotcha laugh. Maybe he called her, said he knew what she did to Sylvia and asked why she came inside and told her maybe she'd like to come back and take a picture like he was having everyone here do.' Elise struggled to make her accusation of Fran real. In her heart did she know that it wasn't Fran who came into the house the night Sylvia was killed?

Elise pressed a hand against her head. 'Dwight laughed. His gonna-see-you-crawl laugh. He saw that woman. I know he did. He didn't care about Sylvia. He didn't care about the police. He thought he'd have fun, show somebody they weren't as smart as they thought. I told him somebody killed Sylvia. You can't fool with someone like that.'

As Mama always told us kids, 'If you poke a tiger, don't turn your back.'

Dwight poked a tiger and the tiger poked back.

Crystal and Jason's suite was empty. I found them downstairs. The pinball room blazed with light. Jason bent close to the machine, his right hand flipping, flipping, lights flashing, the silver ball caroming here and there, Jason shooting, 'Yeah Yeah Yeah.'

Crystal looked small in an oversized chair, small and wizened and frightened.

I Appeared in the empty hallway. Likely Margaret was in her office. Stuart might be at his father's desk in the other wing. He'd looked abstracted earlier, a million things on his mind. I knocked briskly on the game-room door, turned the knob, walked in.

Crystal clutched at the throat of her pale rose warmups. She was on her feet while Jason still hunched at the pinball machine. Flip, flip, flip. She came toward me, a trembling hand outstretched. 'Do you know?' The words were scarcely audible.

'Know?'

'Who killed Dwight.'

Jason sent a ball to one side and it trickled away. He turned, blurted, 'He twisted wrong off the board. The damn show-off got up there and played king of the mountain and it finally got him. He slipped when he bounced and came down and cracked his head. For God's sake, Crystal, nobody killed him.' He skidded to a stop beside her.

'Oh Jason. You always think everything's all right. Like when Mr Baker got you to invest in that mining company. You don't see things.' She didn't sound like a super-confident socialite. She sounded old and sad. And frightened. Her gaze met mine. 'Someone took that pole, the one that fell down, and hit Dwight when he came up from a dive. That's what happened, didn't it?'

I was firm. 'Yes.'

Crystal spoke the names. 'Elise. Stuart. Me. Jason. Margaret.'

Jason grabbed her arm. 'The door to the terrace was open.'

Slowly Crystal shook her head.

'I heard my name.' Margaret was in the doorway, a quizzical look on her face.

There was an instant of silence. Crystal tensed. Jason stared at the floor.

I said blandly, 'I am speaking briefly with everyone this morning.'

Margaret spoke sharply, 'I hope you're making progress.' She cleared her throat. 'Crystal, I have some ideas for the memorial for your father. I'll talk to you later.' She turned away, closed the door behind her.

Crystal was forlorn. 'Do you think she heard me?'

'So what if she did? She knows everybody's upset. Come on, Crystal, let's go upstairs, start packing. I'm taking you home.'

Margaret sat beside me on a small sofa opposite her desk, looked thoughtful, finally shook her head decisively. 'You have to understand that Dwight had an odd sense of humor. That's all it was. Eight fifteen didn't matter. He just seized on it as something fun to do, everybody take a picture of where they were. I don't think anyone minded. It was a . . . I don't know . . . a distraction. A game.' Her eyes narrowed. 'This is a wild guess on my part, but I think Dwight reached out to that woman . . . I can't think of her name. She owns the antique store. She was photographed on the terrace. She had no business to be on the terrace at night. She must have come to meet with Sylvia. We don't know what might have gone on between them. Sylvia was a sharp businesswoman. Maybe she put something on consignment at the shop and they had a disagreement. There will turn out to be something there. Dwight was really interested when he saw the security footage. Maybe he decided to give her a call. It would be just like him. Dwight loved confrontation. Maybe he called her, claimed he knew what happened in the library. It will turn out to be something like that.' Her gaze was demanding. 'I would think the police would have a lot of questions for her. Not for us.'

Fran's kitchen told the tale. A partially cooked frittata was congealed in a skillet pulled from the burner, abandoned on the middle of the stove top. Two mugs half filled with coffee sat by unused plates on the small white wooden table.

Muff twined around one ankle. I bent, stroked her silky black fur. A plaintive mew.

It took a moment to find her food in a plastic container in an alcove. I poured a scoop of pellets into a bowl, refreshed her water bowl. As Stuart Chandler had said, 'Damn Damn. Damn.' I'd counted on Howie Harris waiting until Monday to dredge up a motive for Fran. I counted on her being safe from arrest until then. The kitchen in disarray told me I was wrong.

'Back off or I'll arrest you too.' Howie glared up at Don Smith.

Don loomed over the smaller man. 'She's innocent.' The words shot like rocks from a volcano.

Howie pressed his lips together, turned and walked to his desk in the temporary office. He sat down.

Don remained in the doorway, big, strong, determined.

Howie slowly shook his head. His face reformed in dismay, regret. He spoke quietly. 'I'm sorry you got mixed up with her.' He leaned forward, 'Look, man, we've got her. She was on the terrace Friday night—'

'At eight twenty-two. The murderer re-entered the house at eight fifteen. There's a witness.'

Howie picked up a pen, pulled a legal pad closer. 'Who?'

'The artist. The one who pretended to find her body when he arrived later with a painting. Travis Roberts.'

Howie wrote the name. 'Who interviewed him?'

'Detective Loy.'

'Oh yeah, that agent from OSBI.' Howie sounded matter-of-fact. I blessed tactful Sam. Despite the tense moment, I enjoyed a quick smile. The agent dispatched by, according to Sam, Higher Powers. Howie turned to his computer, clicked, read, turned back to Don. 'Listen man, there's not a damn thing there that makes any difference. For starters, first the artist said he didn't go inside the library, now he claims he did. And so the artist says he heard a door shut. So what? Maybe somebody stepped out for a breath of air, stepped back inside. As for the knobs without fingerprints, maybe somebody had sticky hands, just eaten a caramel, dropped it, picked it up. Hell man, your hands are sticky, you touch something, maybe it was a neat freak, got to wipe the knobs. That doesn't prove anything. Maybe the knobs were wiped the next day. Who knows? Who cares?' Howie pushed back his chair, stood. 'I'll tell you what proves something. It's the fact that her cell phone got a call from Dwight Douglas on the night somebody cracked his head. And we got his cell. The search party found it. I'll tell you what happened. She cracks Douglas's skull, found his cell, ran outside, called herself, kept the call going long enough for those scary whispers, then called nine-one-one and threw the phone over the side of the steps as she got away. Sure, she spins a tale that she's home alone and gets a call and a whispery voice says she has to come to the terrace. Then she calls you, let's you get up there to find the body. As for you, go have a drink. Have a bunch. She's played you for a fool. Now she's here and she knows we've got her cornered. We'll give her a little time to herself, maybe another half-hour in the interrogation room, and we'll see what she has to say.'

Fran sat on a hard wooden straight chair not far from a dingy beige wall. All the walls were dingy. She faced a Formica-topped table with three chairs. The table was scarred from old cigarette burns which indicated its age, a table that had been in the police station for thirty or forty years provided a surface on which inquisitors could place coffee mugs or tall cups of icy Coke while the prisoner's throat dried and a parched tongue felt thick against teeth. A stark fluorescent fixture in the ceiling above her bathed her in an unremitting glare. The cold still room had an odd smell, maybe perspiration, maybe desperation; a room that wasn't aired, a room that embraced anger and fear and despair. She sat on the chair, her hands tightly clasped. Her golden ringlets were carefully brushed and teased, no doubt her wish to be pretty for Don. Her face wasn't pretty now. Her face was empty and hopeless and frightened.

I moved close, whispered. 'Refuse to answer questions. You have the right to one phone call. Call Megan Wynn, attorney-at-law. Tell her Bailey Ruth asked you to contact her.'

She reached out a seeking hand.

I took her hand in both of mine, held tight for an instant, then loosed my grasp.

She managed a wan smile.

I was desperately afraid for Fran. Howie Harris brushed aside the possibility Travis heard the murderer re-enter the house through the red door on Friday night. Howie pointed to the footage from the security tape and the call from Dwight's cell phone to Fran last night.

I felt as though I teetered on the edge of a chasm and Fran and I would plummet down, but that was the last thing I wanted her to know. I spoke in an everyday voice. 'I fed Muff. I'll make sure she's all right. They'll be here in a few minutes. Tell me again about that phone call.'

I listened intently. Whispers. A threat. The order to come to the terrace. Detective Loy could point out to Howie Harris that the most important fact about Dwight Douglas's cell phone was not the call to Fran. What mattered was the fact that Douglas did not take a selfie at eight fifteen. But that argument would seem ephemeral to Howie. I knew Dwight died because he dared to taunt a murderer with the fact that he was leaving the pool at eight fifteen on Friday night and opened the door and saw someone walking swiftly up the hall. Saw a murderer walk swiftly up the hall.

Last night, the murderer took Dwight's cell phone and checked to be sure there was no selfie. And then? The plan, likely a pleasing plan, to try and entice Fran to the site, calling on Dwight's cell. The murderer was keenly aware of time. There was the selfie to be made on his or her cell phone purporting to show the location on Friday night. That required a return to the site for the selfie, taking the selfie at eight fifteen, then making the whispery call and the nine-one-one call. And then easing down the hall and opening the door to the terrace and hurrying to the steps and going down a bit to fling Dwight's cell phone away, confident it would be found in a search the next day. The net would close tight around Fran because the phone was found outside.

I pictured the murderer finally returning to the selfie spot, sinking on to a chair or sofa, breathing fast, palms sweaty, listening for the sound of sirens.

I thought of them all in their selfie spots, Elise and Crystal upstairs in their suites. Jason in the pinball room. Stuart in the dart room, Margaret in her office.

'Fran, imagine you are hearing that whisper. Put your mind back. Listen. What do you hear? I want anything, everything, every slightest sound.'

'The call . . .' She cupped her hands over her ears. Her face tensed. Her eyes squeezed shut. A long moment and her eyes opened and her hands fell to her lap. 'The whisper was breathy, high, the words hissing. The whisper . . . Something . . . yes . . . a funny little sound. A little sound.'

'High?'

She shook her head.

'Tinny?'

Another head shake.

'A pattern?'

She squeezed her eyes shut again. 'No pattern. Just every so often a little sound.'

'Hollow?'

Her eyes stared at the wall. 'Hollow? No. Maybe—'

The door swung in.

FOURTEEN

Howie Harris strode in. His wispy hair might be straggly and untidy, but his gaze was direct and cold and hard. Don, tall and strong, was behind him. Don gave Fran a swift sweet smile and his dark eyes locked with hers. Judy Weitz was the last. She closed the door. In the silence, the sound of that click was freighted with finality. Judy's rounded face was carefully devoid of expression. She didn't look at Fran.

Fran's chin rose. She straightened her slender shoulders, sat tall in the hard chair, but her eyes looked enormous in her still face.

Howie took the center seat behind the old wooden table. Judy Weitz placed a recorder on the table. Don came around the table, took two big steps, grabbed Fran's hands.

Howie was curt. 'Smith, sit down or get out.'

Fran pulled her hands away. "It's all right.'

It wasn't all right, but it was all they had, that reassuring touch, then Don turned away, walked to the table. He pulled out the third chair, scraping the legs against the concrete floor. He sat down and the chair creaked beneath his weight.

Judy turned on the recorder and in a monotone identified the time, the case, the circumstances.

Howie cleared his throat. He pulled a card from his pocket and loudly read the Miranda warning. A pause. 'Tell us about your relationship with Sylvia Chandler.'

Fran spoke firmly. 'I wish to state for your record that I, Frances Mitchell Loring, know nothing about the deaths of Sylvia Chandler and Dwight Douglas. I have not had any contact with Sylvia Chandler in more than three years. I have never had any contact whatsoever with Dwight Douglas. That is my true and complete statement. I decline to answer questions until I have consulted an attorney.'

Howie leaned back in his chair. 'You can make your phone

call. We can hold you for twenty-four hours pending an arrest. You will be escorted to a cell.'

Fran stood in the middle of the cell. There were several cells in the basement of the police station. At mid-afternoon on a Sunday, none of the other cells was occupied.

'Fran,' my tone was urgent. 'You started—'

The heavy steel door at the end of the corridor had a rusty hinge that squealed as it swung in. Don Smith nodded to a jailer. 'Ten minutes. Thanks, Jake.' The door closed.

Don Smith swung around and looked, saw Fran.

She stood at the bars, hands gripping the steel rods.

He was there in an instant. He slipped his arms through the bars, pulled her as near as he could. 'Megan Wynn's on her way. I talked to her. Told her you're innocent.' He paused. His voice was puzzled. 'She told me she knew you were innocent and she'd be there as soon as she dropped the baby off at her mother's.'

'A criminal lawyer with a baby?'

'I don't know how many criminal cases she handles, but she sounded smart. And hey, she said she knows you're on the side of the angels.'

'I don't know about angels.' There was an odd tone in Fran's voice, too. 'I think . . .' And it was as if sunshine broke through heavy dark clouds, 'Oh Don, suddenly I feel that everything's going to be all right.'

'Of course everything's going to be all right.' His voice was deep and confident.

But I could see Don's face, his chin pressed against her golden ringlets. His face was that of a man who sees the rushing, crushing onslaught of an avalanche.

Steel rasped. The guard stepped into the corridor.

Don pulled away far enough to look down at Fran. 'I love you. I know it's too soon but I do. I'll see you through. I promise.' He broke away, started up the corridor, looked back one last time.

Fran managed a smile. 'I'm all right.'

Don turned a hand toward her, then, with a jerk, swung away, walked to the open door.

The guard, a slight man with sparse gray hair and a stoic face, stood aside.

Don stepped through the doorway, stopped to look back.

The older man gave a curious glance at the only occupied cell as he pulled the heavy door. Don moved into the hall.

The steel door slammed shut.

The harsh lights in the corridor slanted into the empty cells and threw the shadows of the bars across the concrete floor where Fran stood.

'Fran.' I spoke softly.

'Can the lawyer get me out of here?' There was a tiny quiver of panic in her voice. She'd kept her composure with Don, but now she was alone in the silence and the musty air.

'She'll be here soon.' I didn't answer directly. I was afraid there might be too much circumstantial evidence for Megan Wynn to get Fran released. But hope is better than fear. 'Right now I need your help. You heard a sound behind the whisper.'

'The whisper and every so often a sound.' Fran shivered. 'I can't be definite. I only heard it a few times. Maybe three. Faint. Erratic. Just a little sound. A' – she paused – 'little sound. That's as near as I can get.'

Detective Loy Appeared in the cramped vestibule of the women's restroom. The mirror would have looked at home in a Boris Karloff castle and likely had last been Windexed a decade ago. I smoothed down several red curls.

Don Smith was pacing in a waiting area at the entrance to the station.

'Detective Smith.' As he turned, I spoke briskly, 'Detective Weitz suggested I ask your help. I'm Special Agent Loy.' I spoke quickly to forestall any awkward questions about OSBI and my assignment. 'I need a recorder to use at the Chandler house. Can you provide a recorder?'

Don nodded. 'I'll get one.' He wheeled away, strode down a corridor, turned out of my sight. He returned in less than two minutes, the small plastic recorder in his right hand.

I slipped the recorder into a rather dull but large leather shoulder bag. 'I've spoken with Mrs Loring.'

He watched me intently.

'There may be a way of identifying who called her on Dwight Douglas's cell phone.'

Hope flared in his watching eyes.

'Will you come with me to the Chandler house?'

The Corvette slid to a stop in the Chandler circular drive. Don followed me up the steps. I rang. Stuart Chandler opened the door. I took the lead. 'We have a few questions, Mr Chandler.' I moved forward.

True to his upbringing, Stuart retreated, holding the door for us to enter.

I was pleasant. 'Here's what we'd like to do . . .'

The door to Elise's suite was open, but I paused on the threshold. 'Mrs Douglas, may we have a few minutes of your time?' I carried the recorder in my right hand, unobtrusively turned it on.

She sat on the plaid sofa, gestured for us to enter. 'Have you arrested her?'

The black bird in the cage near the bedroom door gave a sharp caw.

Don replied. 'Mrs Loring is in custody.'

Elise gave a huge sigh. 'Then it's done.' She brushed a tangle of black curls from the side of her surgically planed face. The bird gave a sharp cry. She looked up. 'It's all right, Sebastian.' She seemed to dismiss us from her thoughts.

I glanced at Don, gave a tiny nod toward the chairs opposite her. He and I sat down. I placed the recorder on my lap.

She looked at me incuriously, then spoke in a rapid monotone. 'I'm going home tomorrow.'

Don was courteous. 'Thank you for granting us a few moments. Mrs Douglas,' the bird cawed three times in succession, 'what time did you last see your husband?'

'A little before a quarter to eight. He always went down to the pool about that time.' Tears brimmed, slid down her tight cheeks. He said, 'This is going to be fun.' She lifted a hand, brushed away the moisture. 'I said,' a pause, a breath, 'I said, 'Dwight, don't leave me. I don't want you to leave me. I'm frightened. Sebastian flapped his wings. He does that sometimes when he wants attention. Dwight pointed at him, said he'd keep me company. Dwight laughed and walked away and then he was gone.'

The bird cawed.

Crystal stood in the hallway outside her suite. As we walked up, she put her hands on her hips. 'You're back and Stuart said Jason had to go back downstairs because of you. I don't like being alone in this house.'

'You're quite safe, Mrs Pace.' I gestured toward the open door. 'We came to reassure you. Let's go inside and we'll explain.'

She whirled and walked into the little living area, dropped on to a chair opposite the sofa. The room was cold, the door to a balcony ajar, the bedroom door ajar. I suspected Crystal Pace always wanted to be out and doing, not cooped up.

I looked at Don, nodded at the sofa. As he joined me, he turned on the recorder.

'Mrs Pace . . .' The clear notes from a wind chime sounded through the open balcony door and I made an instant decision. 'The acting chief of police will be here at seven p.m. tonight to report on the status of the investigation.'

Don turned to look at me, his face a mixture of shock, mystification and alertness.

The wind chimes sang.

In the hall, I walked briskly back toward Elise's suite.

Don tugged at my elbow. 'So who says?'

'I do.' I knocked softly on her door.

The door swung in far enough to reveal her too-smooth face with haunted eyes and black silk blouse and slacks.

'We've just been informed,' I spoke quickly, 'the acting chief of police will be here at seven tonight to report on the status of the investigation.'

'I'll come.' Her tone was harsh. The door shut.

As we reached the first floor, Don looked at me curiously. 'Just been informed? Smoke signals, tom toms, ESP?'

'I have a hunch.' I've long known that telling a man you

have a feeling is wasted effort, but men relate to hunches. 'I've asked Mrs Loring to remember the call from Dwight's cell phone. I may be out on a limb,' I would be out on a limb and tumbling to an ignominious fall if my gamble didn't pay off, 'but there are two facts. The murderer called her because only the murderer could have his phone. The murderer would only make that call in a safe place. We're going to those safe places now. And we're going to listen.' I pointed at the recorder. 'And tape any sounds.'

Don gave a low whistle, with a touch of sheesh-you're-nuts incredulity. 'Lady, if you pull this off, you've got my vote.'

'Vote for what?' We were at the door to Stuart's manly retreat.

'Chutzpah Queen.'

I rather liked that appellation, but quickly suppressed my pleasure. Wiggins would not be amused.

I knocked and Stuart opened the door. He held several darts in his left hand. A target hung on the wall next to the stag's antlers. Two darts were near the center.

I gestured. 'What a pleasure to see a target. I would love to watch you throw.'

'I've had a lot of practice ever since Dwight started that selfie thing.' He gave a little shrug and faced the target.

Don clicked on the recorder.

Thump. Thump. Thump. Stuart retrieved the darts, moved back, Thump.

'Did you see Dwight when you came down here to take your selfie?'

Stuart was poised to throw. A hesitation. The dart wobbled in its flight, skittered off the target to the floor. 'That one's a little off balance.' He threw again, hit the bull's eye. 'Dwight and I walked down the hall together. He was still heading for the pool room when I stepped in here, shut the door. The last time I saw him.'

Don looked interested. 'How did he appear?'

Stuart rubbed the side of his face. 'Fine. Best of spirits. He loved to dive.'

I took a step nearer. 'Did you see anyone else in the hall?'

'No.'

'Thanks for your help.' Don went into the hall. I said without inflection. 'The acting chief will be here at seven tonight to report on the investigation.'

I didn't bother to knock at the game room. I turned the knob and we walked in.

Jason was intent at the big pinball machine, lights flashing. His right hand worked the lever. Flip. Flip. Flip.

Don turned on the recorder.

Flip. Flip Flip. The sound was quick, erratic. No pattern.

'We won't interrupt your game, Mr Pace. Please keep on playing.' I stood beside the machine.

'OK. What's up?' He paused, gave me a quick look. 'No more bodies?'

'Just a few questions. Please keep playing. Did you see Dwight after dinner?'

He gazed at the machine. Flip. Flip. 'Nope. Oh, I saw him head down the stairs so I hung back a little. I was getting damn tired of all the eight fifteen stuff. But Crystal and I don't pick fights.' Flip. Flip. Flip. 'Hey.' The ball caromed and lights blazed. 'Got that one.' He let his hand drop, stood straighter.

'That's all we needed.' I nodded at Don and he started for the door. I looked back from the threshold. 'Please be down-stairs at seven tonight. The acting police chief will be here to report on the investigation.'

'Good to know,' he called after us. 'Crystal and I are out of here tomorrow.' He looked almost buoyant

'After dinner?' Margaret Foster picked up the pencil, rolled it in her fingers, held it between thumb and forefinger, tapped the desktop. Tap. Tap. Tap.

I pointed at the door. 'Perhaps you saw him in the hall.'

'No.' A slight frown. 'I thought I heard voices,' several taps, 'but I'm not sure. I keep my window ajar usually. A squirrel was making his evening commentary, likely complaining that someone put a metal cover over the bird feeder.'

I kept on point. 'Did you speak with Dwight?'

Now she was definite. 'I spoke to no one after dinner. I was here' – Tap. Tap. – 'until Elise screamed.' A shaken look. 'That scream . . .'

I leaned forward. 'Mrs Foster, you've been associated with the Chandler family for many years. Who do you suspect?'

She was jolted. 'Oh no. No.'

I stood. 'Tonight at seven' – Don rose, turned toward the door, carrying the recorder – 'the acting chief will address the family.'

The Corvette pulled up in front of City Hall, which housed the police department.

Don's hands were clenched on the steering wheel. 'No warning? No prep?' The question bristled with outrage.

'I know what I'm doing.' I dearly hoped I did. Oh yes, I hoped so.

Don's hard voice was loud, furious. 'Roust her out of a cell, haul her to that damn house? If they put handcuffs on her—'

'No handcuffs.'

'Just how the hell do you think you can tell Howie Harris what to do?'

'On a wing and a prayer,' I murmured.

Don's expression was blank. Those long-ago words from World War II meant nothing to him; didn't evoke a flak-weakened, mangled wing and a bomber gliding just long enough to make it back over the Channel to England.

I opened the door. 'Bring Travis and Jennifer Roberts.'

'So I show up on their doorstep and say pretty please come with me?'

'They will come. Tell them Detective Loy expects them.'

Judy's Weitz's right hand hovered over the donuts in a lopsided box on the break-room table. 'Chocolate custard. Howie's favorite.' She chose two, slid them on to a paper plate. 'And Mountain Dew.'

To each his own. But if this combo pleased Howie, I would present it as if nectar to the gods.

Judy looked inquiring. 'What would you like?'

'Coffee. Is there any real milk?'

She laughed. 'Not in this cop shop. Creamers.'

'Black, then.' I picked up the tray.

As I reached the door, she said softly, 'Safe landing.'

I knew she'd talked to Don.

I took a deep breath outside Howie Harris's temporary office, donned a smile. I knocked on the partially open door and the panel swung in.

FIFTEEN

Howie turned a legal pad face down, looked up with a frown.

'Chief Harris, I'm Special Agent Loy.' I held out the tray. 'I did a little detecting and I've brought a snack, your favorite donuts.' I crossed the few feet and placed the tray on the desk. 'Chocolate custard donuts and Mountain Dew. Chief Cobb has been most courteous. He sends his warm regards. He is very impressed with your excellent work on the homicides at the Chandler house.'

The frown disappeared, replaced by a modest glow. Howie was still in his golf clothes, a mauve polo shirt and navy Bermuda shorts.

I settled in a straight chair facing his desk. I picked up a coffee mug. 'A toast to you as we complete a successful investigation.'

Howie spoke around a mouthful of donut. 'Complete?'

'This evening at seven o'clock at the Chandler house. Here's what we will do . . .'

At a quarter to seven I stepped into the Pritchard Mausoleum. I'd borrowed a small flashlight from Fran's house when I fed Muff, petted her, told her Fran would soon be there to hold her and love her. I spent a quarter-hour on the settee, stroking soft fur, murmuring promises.

Am I superstitious? Absolutely not. Never. Well, only a tad. And what harm did it do to flick on the light in that cold, cold mausoleum and stroke the cat's whiskers and pet the lean greyhound? It was like an actress a few minutes before the knock on the door. I'd be on stage at the Chandler house in only a few minutes and—

Coal smoke swirled. Cinders sparked. Wheels thundered on steel rails.

I saw Wiggins in the thin slice of light from the flash. 'Wiggins.' Did I sound panicked?

'Sorry to be in a rush.' The Express gave an emphatic whoo. 'I know you feel at home with dogs and cats. Even if they're marble. Quite a crisis in Tumbulgum. Missing jewels on a houseboat holiday and I must make sure that sweet young nanny is exonerated. Must hurry back.' Wheels thundered, coal smoke thickened, cinders flared. 'Remember your most important mission. Don and . . .' He was gone.

'I definitely will,' I shouted after him, in huge relief that I wasn't being yanked aboard the caboose. 'Of course. Don and . . .' I certainly would do what I could to erase a reprimand from Don's record, secure his promotion, but right now I needed a burst of confidence to see me through the coming evening. I stepped first to the cat, stroked her cold whiskers. 'Make Fran free tonight.' I took three steps, patted the grey-hound's shoulder, said rather helplessly but with definite hope, 'Don and . . .'

Brilliant light cascaded from the three chandeliers in the huge living area, revealing the frayed edges of a tapestry with a weary wayfarer in a plain gray robe and worn leather sandals straining up a mountain path, the film of dust on a marble-topped table, and the imprint of stress and fear on wary faces.

Elise Douglas was pale with dark pouches beneath grieving eyes. Black hair, black clothing, black world. Bright red nails were the only touch of color. Crystal's rose warmups, perfect for tennis, were a bright contrast, but her blue eyes were haunted and the blonde hair in a ponytail was at odds with pinched features. Jason was seated but mobile, flexing his hands and feet. His country-club-perfect appearance, thick blond hair, handsome face, tidy mustache, were a stark contrast to Elise's misery. Stuart looked more attentive than apprehensive, comfortably wearing the mantle of the man of the house. Thinning hair neatly brushed, no flush from whisky. Instead of sweats, a cream polo shirt, khakis, loafers. Margaret's V-neck black cardigan was saved from severity by the red trim on the lapels and hem. The red-and-black striped blouse was another touch of color. Black slacks. Her lean face, framed by short gray hair, looked uncertain, as if she felt out of place. Perhaps that's why she sat a little apart from the family in a plain card-table chair. Perhaps she saw herself as an employee, not really involved.

The front door opened. Don Smith held the door wide for Jennifer and Travis Roberts. Don carried the small black recorder in his right hand. Jennifer's blue eyes were huge. Her soft brown hair was carefully brushed and she wore a pale green silk dress and heels. All dressed up to visit the King's Road house? Travis's angular face was freshly shaved and his overlong hair drawn back in a neat man bun. He looked sporty in a beige crew-neck sweater and brown slacks.

Don unfolded chairs for Jennifer and Travis, placed them near Margaret.

A grandfather clock bonged the hour as the front door opened again. Judy Weitz was spruced up in a navy silk dress. I winced at the black shoes. Thankfully Fran was not in jail garb. Her thin face was wan, but her candy-striped sweater and rose wool slacks were attractive. Her dark eyes moved uncertainly from face to face and then she saw Don. A look, a pause, and a moment of sun in her gaze.

Travis jumped up, held out a big hand. 'Fran, what are you doing here?'

Judy surveyed the faces turned toward Fran. 'Mrs Loring is assisting the investigation.'

'It's all right, Travis.' Fran's clear voice was steady.

'All right? Nothing's right.' Elise Douglas jumped to her feet, stretched out a shaking hand. 'You're the one. You were on the terrace. You killed Sylvia. You killed my husband.' Elise started across the terrazzo tiled floor, crimson-nailed hands outstretched, shoes staccato against stone.

Jason moved fastest, clutched her arm. 'Take a breath. Hey, take a breath.'

Fran stepped forward. 'I never met your husband. I never spoke to him. When I answered that call from what turned out to be his cell phone, I'd just taken an apple pie out of the oven.'

Every woman in the room thought of apple pie, making a pie. What woman would bake an apple pie and kill a man?

I moved close to Elise. 'Mrs Loring is innocent.'

Tears edged down Elise's cheeks. She was scarcely able to stand, held on to Jason's arm. 'Who killed Dwight?'

Jason gently moved her toward her chair.

I spoke directly to Elise. 'Your husband saw the murderer Friday night in the hallway outside the pool. Your husband knew the murderer. Your husband did not know Mrs Loring.'

Her haggard face was piteous. 'Someone here?' She looked from face to face, Crystal, Jason, Stuart, Margaret.

No one spoke. No one moved. The silence was as icy and foreboding as wind off a glacier.

The front door opened. I announced as if presenting a royal personage, 'Acting Chief Howie Harris has arrived.'

If Howie enjoyed being a focal point, this was his moment. He, too, dressed for King's Road, a gray pinstripe suit that gave him dignity.

I walked to meet him, shepherded him to a space between a Goya and a suit of armor. I faced the room. 'It is my honor tonight to represent Acting Chief Harris. He has overseen the investigation from its beginnings. He cleverly took advantage of Mrs Loring's accidental arrival on the terrace to suggest the murderer was a stranger to the house.' Howie's face stiffened. I talked faster. 'Friday night Travis Roberts called Sylvia Chandler to discuss next summer's art festival. She and Mr Roberts weren't in agreement on the artists to be invited. Sylvia was the festival judge and had sole discretion in the selection of artists.'

Travis Roberts's angular face came alive. 'Everything's set for the festival. I talked to the woman who's taking over. We got everything arranged.'

His monumental self-concern wasn't fazed by murder or the search for a murderer. First things first and his paintings would always be first for Travis.

I gave him a bright smile. 'Mr Roberts has been extremely helpful to the authorities.'

'Yeah.' It was as if he came back to the big room from a far distance. No doubt he was picturing his painting that was perfect for the festival poster. 'Glad to help.'

'The information he provided is critically important. Mr Roberts, describe your arrival on the Chandler terrace.'

Travis cleared his throat. 'I called Mrs Chandler to discuss the summer arts festival. I had a painting I wanted to show her but it was at the gallery so I started off in my car. Then I decided to talk to her first. I stopped halfway up the hill. I went through the woods to the terrace stairs.'

My smile never wavered. Some truth, some deception, but Travis could be expected to put himself in a good light. There was no hint of aggrieved artist storming up to demand his due.

'I ran up the steps to the terrace. The door to the library was wide open. I stepped inside, called out for her. I figured she'd gone somewhere for a minute. I decided to take a look at another painting and when I walked close to the fireplace,' his voice fell, 'I saw her all crumpled up on the couch. God, it was awful. I panicked and wanted to get away, not see the blood. All of a sudden I was out on the terrace. I didn't know what to do. I thought I needed to get help. I was about to go back inside and then I heard a door shut. There are three doors from the terrace into the house. The library door. A yellow door that goes into the kitchen. And a red door at the end of the west wing. I couldn't see the red door because the whole west wing was in dark shadows. But I heard a click and I knew it was the red door. Somebody,' his eyes were dark with remembered shock, 'went into the house. When I heard that door shut, I ran. Somehow I got back to my car and I thought I had to do something. By that time I was at the gallery and I got the painting and I thought I would show up and say it was for Sylvia because she couldn't just be left there, lying in all that blood.'

I summed up his statement. 'Mr Roberts heard the red door into the house shut and, thanks to his wife, Jennifer, we know that door shut at eight fifteen.'

Jennifer Roberts, looking young and earnest like a camp counselor organizing activities, said eagerly, 'Well, it is just such a good thing I was out with our dog.' She gestured to her left. 'We live at the foot of the hill. After Travis left, Buddy had to go outside and he got all excited and sniffed and tugged me toward the hill. I went up the steps. I tied his leash to the railing. But there was something scary about the lights on the terrace and I though oh, I'd better go home, and I hurried down the stairs. All of a sudden I heard running footsteps. And just at that moment my cell-phone reminder for Buddy's pills sounded so I know the footsteps were at exactly eight fifteen because that's when my phone chimed. And then I saw Travis and I didn't know what to think. He was running so fast. Bless his heart. No wonder he was upset. Why, Mrs Chandler had been such a boost to his career and he thought the world of her. Seeing Travis run was so upsetting I just flew home. But my sister-in-law,' she pointed at Fran, 'was at our house when I took Buddy out and after a while she came out I guess to get in her car and go home and I think she heard Buddy so she came up the hill to help. And she found Buddy but he got away from her and she chased him down the hillside and bless her little heart she fell into the pond and so did Buddy, they were both soaking when she came back to the house. But anyway Fran didn't come outside until Travis had already gone to the gallery so when she came to the terrace Mrs Chandler was already dead so Fran—'

I interrupted. 'Thank you, Mrs Roberts. Clearly Mrs Chandler was dead before Mrs Loring arrived. The great importance of your testimony and your husband's is the fact that the red door into the house closed at eight fifteen. Mr Roberts called Mrs Chandler at shortly after eight. The murder occurred between the time he spoke to her and his arrival on the terrace. A crime technician examined the knobs on the red door that opens to the hall by the pool. There were no fingerprints Saturday on either the outer or inner knob. The murderer re-entered the house at eight fifteen and polished those knobs. Chief Harris,' I gave him an approving nod, hoped his congealed expression didn't indicate indigestion resulting from chocolate custard donuts, 'knew then that the murderer was a resident of Chandler house.' I looked at each in turn. 'That brings us to the murder of Dwight Douglas.'

Elise gripped the wooden chair arms.

'At eight fifteen Friday evening, Dwight Douglas opened the door from the pool and watched the murderer hurry up the hallway.'

Elise's head moved as she gazed in turn at Crystal, Jason, Stuart and Margaret.

'Dwight thrived on excitement. He knew that only he and Sylvia's murderer understood the significance of each person's location at eight fifteen. He devised an entertainment. Everyone would take a selfie of their whereabouts at that moment. Perhaps he looked knowingly at the murderer at several points during the day on Saturday. I saw you . . . He knew everyone would take the selfie and one would be a lie but he would have that special knowledge and enjoy every moment.'

'I warned him.' Elise's broken cry came from deep in her throat.

'Saturday night Dwight strode down the hall to the pool door. He intended to follow the rules of his game, take his selfie at the appointed time as he departed after his swim. He would hold up the cell phone and snap himself in the doorway looking up the hallway. But first he would swim. He dropped his robe, the cell phone in the pocket, on a deckchair.'

Elise began to tremble.

'We can picture his last moments. Dwight dives from the high board. The murderer, holding a rescue pole, attacks as he comes to the surface. The murderer dips the pole in the water to wash away blood—'

Elise shuddered.

'—then hurries around the end of the pool to return the pole to its brackets. Now a search for his cell phone. Dwight's robe is lying on a deckchair. The phone is in the pocket. A quick check to make sure there was no early bird selfie. The murderer carefully eases open the hall door. Listens. No sound. No movement. Hurry, hurry, hurry. The murderer steps into the hall, closes the door. Quickly to the terrace door. Perhaps using a handkerchief or the edge of a sweater, the murderer opens the door to the terrace. Opening the door takes only an instant and then a whirl and rush to get out of the hall. Everyone is supposed to be at their selfie spot. The murderer reaches that special place and shuts the door; Dwight's cell phone is in one hand. The murderer stares at the phone. The door to the terrace is open but it would be even better to use Dwight's cell to increase suspicion of Fran Loring. The whispery call is made to try and entice Fran to come to the terrace. Now there would be a record of a call from Dwight's phone on her cell phone. Then a call to nine-one-one and a frantic hoarse cry for help for a drowning victim. Finally, a careful inspection of the hall, still empty, and a rush to the door and out into the night to fling Dwight's phone into the woods.'

I glanced at Fran. 'Tell us about the call.'

Her face held remembered terror. 'The caller whispered, threatened me, demanded I come to the terrace. Then there was silence. I immediately called Detective Don Smith and he told me to stay home and lock the doors.'

Don nodded. 'After I received her call, I drove to the Chandler house. I approached through the woods. As I reached the terrace, I saw the red door was open. I heard screams.'

'After killing Dwight, the murderer returned to the selfie spot. The call to Fran on Dwight's phone occurred at eight thirty-two. Chief Harris' – Howie looked startled and wary – 'agrees that the call made on Dwight's phone was the murderer's critical error.'

Harris's mouth was agape.

'At eight thirty-two Margaret is in her office, Stuart is in the dart room, Jason is in the pinball room, Crystal is upstairs in her suite, Elise is in her suite. Picture the murderer safely returned to the selfie spot. No one to see. No one to hear. Looking at Dwight's cell and the exciting decision. Call the antique lady.'

Margaret might have been graven in stone, utterly intent. Stuart's pudgy hands lifted slightly as if warding away unthinkable images. Jason moved uncomfortably, flexed his fingers again and again. Crystal pressed a soft hand against her lips and a bright emerald gleamed in its ornate setting. Elise's hands tightened into claws.

'The murderer's safe space is familiar, comfortable, used so often that any background noise is no longer heard.' I thought of each safe space and its distinctive sound. The big black bird observed and cawed in Elise's suite. Wind chimes played a tinkling melody for Crystal. Margaret erratically tapped a pencil. Stuart aimed darts that thunked into a target. Jason rapidly worked a lever to light up the pinball machine. I turned to Don. 'Detective Smith.'

Tall, rangy, athletic, Don looked powerful in a black turtleneck, jeans and black sneakers. He moved to the center of the area ringed by chairs. 'Police work often depends upon witnesses. What they saw. What they smelled. In this particular case Fran Loring listened to a whisper. We asked her to focus on the memory of that call. Was there any noise in the background? Mrs Loring has tried to describe an erratic sound that occurred several times during the call. Tonight for the first time she will hear a recording of sounds that occurred in the safe spaces described by Detective Loy. Mrs Loring, please come forward.'

Fran rose, walked slowly to join him. She looked small standing beside him, small but gallant.

Don held up the black plastic recorder. 'Five sounds from five safe places.' He stepped nearer and now the recorder was perhaps a foot away from Fran. He flicked a switch.

Fran lifted a hand to her throat. She stared unseeing at the frayed medieval tapestry.

Five times there was a separate, distinctive sound followed by silence. The sounds in order:

Caw. Caw. A pause. Caw, caw.

Winds chimes tinkled. A moment of quiet. Chime.

Thump. Thump. Thump. Several seconds passed. Thump. Thump.

Flip. Flip. Faster, flip, flip, flip. Flip.

Tap. Tap. A pause. Tap. Tap. Tap.

Fran took a deep breath. 'A little sound. Just a little sound. Very faint. Tap. Tap. Tap. That's what I heard.'

All the family looked at Margaret.

Elise bolted to her feet, took a step. Stuart was there to grip her arm.

Margaret Foster's aura of command and competence was unchanged, but her face was hard, as if sculpted from stone. 'Nonsense.' A dismissive look at Fran. 'What an absurd performance.'

Jennifer Roberts turned her slightly vacant stare on Margaret. 'Fran never lies. If Fran says she heard that noise behind the whisper, then she heard that noise.'

I gazed at Margaret, gestured at the shocked observers.

'Everyone recognized that sound. When you are in your office and thinking hard or perhaps concerned or worried, you pick up a pencil and strike the desktop. Tap. Tap. Tap. No pattern. Tap. Tap. Your stress has been enormous this past week. Sylvia was close to selling the company. The papers in her desk indicate the two sides would meet next Wednesday for final negotiations. The company you loved more than anything in the world, the company you helped build, gone. If Sylvia had lived another week, Chandler Oil would be no more. You killed her and you lied to Stuart, told him Sylvia changed her mind. I expect the family may be interested in talking to the buyers—'

'No.' A visceral cry. She rose from the chair, an animal at bay, ridden by fury. 'All she cared about was money.' Margaret took a step, reached out to Stuart. 'Don't sell the company. Don't.'

SIXTEEN

'It seems like old times.' Sam Cobb poked a chunk of his waffle into a mound of whipped cream.

I smiled at him, grateful for his solid presence, a big strong man with a kind heart. I smiled at my plate, loaded with Lulu's breakfast steak and scrambled eggs and hash browns. Perhaps a bit hearty but I felt entitled. 'A near thing for Fran Loring, but all's well that ends well. And speaking of Shakespeare, I have an idea about Howie.'

Sam listened with an odd expression on his large face. 'The mayor's news conference is in five minutes. I'll make a special announcement. And,' Sam laughed, 'I look forward to being introduced to Detective Loy, the special agent from OSBI.'

'I hate to disappoint you but she's turned in her report, which emphasizes the excellent leadership of Acting Chief Harris, and left town. I'll be on the platform. But you won't see me.'

'Like I said,' Sam grinned, 'just like old times.'

Mayor Neva Lumpkin beamed at the reporters gathered in City Hall's small auditorium, nodded graciously to city officials in attendance. '. . . and I will conclude by commending Acting Chief Howie Harris for a successful and swift – which saves taxpayers' money – conclusion to the shocking crimes that occurred at the Chandler home this past weekend. The Chandler family has also expressed gratitude to Chief Harris.'

Sam clapped. Howie's cheeks turned pink. The mayor smiled. Sam held out a big hand for the microphone. The mayor's eyes narrowed, but with TV cameras whirring, she managed a brilliant smile and relinquished the microphone.

Sam looked every inch a police chief: thick graying hair, big broad face, massive shoulders. His brown suit appeared freshly pressed.

'Returning to work after a leave of absence, it is especially gratifying to know that the police department has been in good hands. You've heard this morning the details of the investigation ably directed by my acting chief. I would like to announce a special recognition to honor Howie Harris. This will be an honor unique to the Adelaide, Oklahoma police department.' Sam boomed, 'In recognition of his extensive creative success in writing poetry, Detective Howie Harris will now be deemed the Adelaide Oklahoma Police Department Poet Laureate.' Sam reached into a capacious pocket of his brown suit, pulled out a clump of tissue, removed the wrappings. 'Howie, this is for you.'

Howie scrambled to his feet from the chair on one side of the mayor. His eyes were huge. He walked to Sam, held out his hand, squinted to peer at Sam's big printing on a white card: Poet Laureate Howie Harris will receive a ceramic bust of Mark Twain to mark his ascension to creative heights in poetry.

Howie gazed at Sam with trembling lips. 'A Mark Twain bust?'

'The bust hasn't arrived yet.'

Since Sam and I created the honor only this morning, I was quite sure the bust had yet to be ordered. But the bust would be ordered.

Sam's smile was huge. 'The bust is for your desk, Poet Laureate Howie Harris.'

I was at the end of the pier in White Deer Park when the red Corvette wheeled into the lot. Don and Fran piled out and came together to walk hand in hand toward the pier. The day was gorgeous, fluffy white clouds in a pale blue sky. The cool wind out of the northeast ruffled Don's thick dark hair, tugged at his beige windbreaker and faded jeans. The wind stirred Fran's golden ringlets. She buttoned her pink jacket. She carried a white sack. Don carried a cup holder in one hand, a backpack dangled from the other.

At the end of the pier, he balanced the drink holder on a post. Fran placed the sack on the next post, gave a tiny shiver.

Don moved near her, looking concerned. 'Are you warm enough? Maybe it's nutty to bring a picnic here in November.'

She looked up at him, her eyes happy, her face soft. 'Not nutty. Fun. You make everything fun.'

His face lighted. 'I want you to be happy.' He took the backpack in both hands, unzipped it. He reached inside, pulled out two large tissue-wrapped objects, began to pull away the paper to reveal two gray leather ankle boots. He held one in each hand, turned them toward her.

'Oh Don. Oh Don. My boots.' She took the boots and held them close to her and then moved to him and he wrapped his arms around her.

Smoke swirled. Cinders glowed. Wheels thundered. The Rescue Express swooped down. I grabbed the railing of the caboose.

Wiggins grasped my arm, brought me safely aboard. 'Well done, Bailey Ruth. And you achieved your most important task.'

'My most important task?' I hoped Don's job was safe. Surely Howie Harris's delight in serving as Poet Laureate of the Adelaide, Oklahoma Police Department would sweep away his rancor toward Don.

Wiggins leaned over the railing, gazed at Fran in Don's arms. 'Don and Fran.' Wiggins's brown eyes twinkled as he turned to me. 'Love is what matters, Bailey Ruth. Yes, now and always it will be Don and Fran.'

I looked down too and my heart sang. Don and Fran. I touched my fingers to my lips, blew a kiss to Don and Fran. 'Fare well, sweet souls.'